CRACKILTON

Crackilton

a novel by

S.E. Tomas

A CREATESPACE BOOK

ISBN-13: 978-1522885627
ISBN-10: 1522885625

1

I was in the passenger seat of my mom's car, heading south on Highway 2 to Edmonton International Airport, when the craving first started. It came on suddenly and for no apparent reason. One minute, I was calmly looking out the window at a snow-covered field alongside the highway, thinking about the trip home, and the very next, all I could think about was doing a really big blast of crack.

At first I tried to ignore the thought. I hadn't smoked crack for three weeks while I was in Edmonton. The last thing I wanted to do was to start smoking it again. The craving was intense, though. Even after my mom had dropped me and Emily, my five-year-old daughter, off at the airport, and we'd checked our luggage, gone through airport security, and boarded the plane, I was still thinking about getting high.

As time went on, the craving only got worse. After a

while, it started to affect my concentration. I tried to watch a show on the seatback television during the flight to pass the time, but the urge to get high was so distracting that I could barely even follow the plot. I started to feel extremely edgy. I kept thinking about getting some dope and putting a rock onto the end of my stem. I kept imagining the way I'd always feel after doing the first hit. It literally made me break out in a cold sweat.

By the time we were an hour away from Pearson Airport in Toronto, I was jonesing so bad. I no longer cared about how I hadn't smoked crack for three weeks, or how I'd told myself before going to Edmonton that I wasn't going to smoke it anymore. For a second, I forgot that I even had my daughter with me. All I wanted to do, as soon as the plane landed, was rush back to Hamilton as fast as I could so that I could get some dope and get high.

When the plane finally landed, I picked up our luggage in the baggage claim area, jumped in a cab, and took Emily back to my ex-girlfriend Nicole, who lived in Toronto. After doing that, I got into my car, which I'd parked at Nicole's place on my way to Edmonton, and then drove to Mississauga to pick up Christine, my girlfriend. Christine had been staying at her parents' over the Christmas holidays. She was a graduate student at McMaster University, where she also worked as a teaching assistant, and had been on her break from school.

I was hoping that it would be a quick stop at Christine's parents' house, but I had no such luck. Christine's parents had made a big dinner that night and they insisted that Christine and I go to the fridge and grab whatever food we wanted to take home with us. It was a nice gesture, but at that moment, I wanted to get high so badly that every second that delayed it was unbearable. Without being rude, I helped Christine get some leftovers out of the fridge as quickly as possible, made sure to say thank you to Christine's mom and dad, and then we got out of there.

It took about half an hour to get to Hamilton from Mississauga. The roads were dry and it was late at night, so there wasn't much traffic on the QEW. The entire way, I drove twenty to thirty kilometers per hour over the speed limit. I would have driven even faster, but every time I tried to Christine got nervous and told me to slow down.

My plan when I got off the freeway in Hamilton was to drop Christine off at home and then go get some dope. Christine didn't know that I still smoked crack—it was a habit that she'd thought I'd quit when we first got together—so I had to make up a bullshit reason for why I was taking off.

"Baby, I'm just going to drop you off, OK?" I said, as we were approaching our building. "I want to go get some weed."

Christine looked at me and sighed. "Do you really have to do that tonight?" she said. "It's almost midnight, Jim. I thought we'd spend some time together before going to bed."

"Yeah, I already called my weed guy," I said. "He'll get pissed off at me if I tell him now that I'm not coming over."

Christine let it go without an argument. When we got to our building, on Ottawa Street, I dropped her off and then went to see Chester, the old guy that I went to to get crack in Hamilton.

It didn't take long for me to get to Chester's. He lived about five minutes away, on Barton Street, near Ivor Wynne Stadium. Barton was a main drag and the longest street in Hamilton, but a really long stretch of it, which included the area by the stadium, was really run-down with a lot of boarded-up storefronts. It was generally known as the place to go in Hamilton if you were looking for drugs or hookers.

When I got to Barton Street, I parked in a vacant lot and then walked over to Chester's building. Chester lived in behind a store, so his door opened right onto the street.

A few seconds after I'd knocked on Chester's door, the door opened. "Oh, hey, Jim," Chester said, looking a little surprised to see me. "Long time no see."

I hadn't seen Chester for a while because before my trip to Edmonton, I'd been getting my dope from a crack dealer whose phone number I no longer had. Chester didn't actually sell dope; he just acted as a middleman. He'd hook you up with a dealer and give you a place to smoke if you needed one.

Chester let me into his tiny, dirty apartment. We walked through the kitchen into a living room area, where there was a couch, a few chairs, and a coffee table in front of an old television set. At the back of the room, in a corner, was a single bed. Sometimes there were a lot of people sitting around, smoking crack in this room. Chester let people get high at his place all the time in exchange for crack. On this particular night, however, the place was empty. I didn't even see Sal around, Chester's roommate.

On the TV, Chester had a porn show playing. He'd been in the middle of watching it and getting high when I'd come to the door. Chester was the type of person who always got a sex buzz when he smoked crack. He almost always had a porn show on whenever I went over there.

I knew that I'd have to wait for Chester to finish smoking his shit before we could go out and meet the dealer, so right away I asked where Sal was. Sometimes if Chester was busy, or if he wasn't home, I'd go out with Sal to meet the dealer. I was hoping that Sal was just down the street, getting a pack of smokes or something, but as it turned out, he wasn't.

"Sal's at his girlfriend's," Chester told me. "We'll go as soon as I finish this, OK?"

I groaned quietly and sat down on Chester's couch. Like everything else in the apartment, it was filthy and was covered in a layer of grime that you could feel on your hands as soon as you touched it. I knew that it wouldn't be long before we'd get to leave the apartment, I was just jonesing so bad, and the apartment was so nasty and gross-smelling because of all the trash that was piled up everywhere from people constantly coming over to hang out and smoke crack, that it annoyed me that I had to wait.

Twenty minutes of sitting there turned out to be all that I could take. The breaking point came when I heard a rustling sound coming from the huge pile of trash over by the coffee table. I looked down, expecting to see a rat by my shoes, and then sat up a little straighter.

"Hey, Chester," I said.

Chester had finished the piece he was smoking and was now just sitting there, watching his show.

"Are you going to call this guy or what?" I said. "I'm tired of waiting, man. Come on, call him already. You can watch this shit later. I want to get going. It's late."

By the way that I was acting, you'd think that I'd already smoked some crack. Once you smoke it, you're extremely eager to get more and you don't want to have to wait to get it. I'd had this craving for so many hours, though, that I just couldn't wait any longer. I'd reached my limit for waiting.

Chester didn't seem to be too concerned about how eager I was to leave the house. He stared at the TV for another ten seconds and then slowly reached for his phone. "How much do you want?" he asked me. "Four?"

"Yeah, four," I said.

Forty dollars' worth was my usual amount. No matter how much money I had on me, which was never much since the carnival season had ended a few months earlier and I'd started working temp jobs—I'd worked under the table that season and therefore wasn't eligible to collect Employment Insurance benefits—forty dollars was about as much as I usually wanted to blow at any given time. I knew that I'd get through a forty piece pretty fast, but I also knew that by then I'd be far too paranoid, thinking the cops would be coming to bust down my door, to drive back to Chester's in the middle of the night to get more. That's how I always got whenever I smoked crack—totally paranoid. I didn't used to get so paranoid when I smoked crack, or freebase, as a kid. But at some point, it just started to happen. Chester wasn't like that, though. He didn't get paranoid. He had no problem leaving the house.

Chester spoke to the dealer briefly and then flipped his phone closed.

"Where are we meeting this guy?" I said.

"Gage and King," Chester said. "He's going to meet us at the convenience store in about ten minutes."

Chester got his ass up off the couch and then we finally left the apartment. We walked over to my car and then drove to the twenty-four-hour convenience store on Gage and King, which was only a couple of minutes away, to meet the dealer.

After waiting for about twenty minutes, the crack man finally showed up. He came up to the passenger side of my car, tapped on the window, and got into the backseat behind Chester.

A gust of cold air rushed into the backseat. It crept up the back of my neck. I turned to the dealer in my seat and gave him the money. The dealer handed me the dope. It was wrapped in a piece of plastic and tied off in a knot. Two seconds later, the back door opened and the dealer took off down King Street.

While we were still in the parking lot, I took a ten-dollar bill out of my pocket and gave it to Chester, like I usually did for a tip. I always gave him money instead of breaking off a piece of dope because I didn't like to open the bag until I got home. It was a hassle and it took too much time.

Once that was settled, I drove back to Chester's house to drop Chester off. After that, I headed home. Even though home was only a short distance away, it felt a lot further because all of a sudden, I really needed to take a shit. Having to shit was from the anticipation of having dope on me and knowing that in a few minutes I'd be smoking it. It happened every time I was about to smoke crack.

When I got home, I parked in the lot at the back of our building and ran up the wooden staircase to our apartment on the third floor. Christine had left the kitchen light on for me. I peered into the living room. It was dark and empty.

I took off my coat and went straight into the bathroom. When you walked into our place, the bathroom was directly to your left, as soon as you walked into the living room. It was a small four-piece with a toilet directly behind the door. The lock on the door was broken and the knob itself was almost falling off, so it was good being able to sit behind the door like that, on the toilet. It gave me a few seconds to react if I needed it.

Once I was in the bathroom, I opened the window a crack, put the bathmat up against the bottom of the door, and then grabbed my crack stem. My stem was literally just a piece of copper pipe about four inches long that I'd found one day at a temp job. Most people who smoked crack used glass stems, but I never knew where to buy glass in Hamilton. I just used whatever I could find. To prevent burning my lips when the metal heated up under the flame, I'd wrapped some electrical tape around one end of the stem. Christine thought that I used the stem to smoke weed, which was totally plausible and which I actually did sometimes, so I didn't have to hide it from her. I had in on the bathroom shelf, in plain sight, next to my shaving kit.

As soon as my stem was in hand, I sat down on the toilet and took a shit. I'd barely eaten anything all day, so there wasn't much in my system. I basically just peed out my ass for a few seconds.

While I sat there on the toilet, I tore off the knot in the plastic, took the dope out, broke off a chunk with my thumbnail—about ten dollars' worth—and then put it onto the end of my stem, on top of my screen. My screen was just a piece of a stainless steel scouring pad that Christine had in the kitchen. After melting the dope into my screen a little bit, I did a really big blast, inhaling as much as I could while holding my stem upwards. Before I'd exhaled, I was already high.

The first sensation felt like I was looking out a window. I felt like I was so close to it that my nose was almost touching the glass. My heart rate jacked up. I started to sweat. My vision got blurry. I felt like there was water running down the other side of the glass, over my face. I heard this *whoosh* sound shoot out of each ear—a ringer, it's called—and then my hearing intensified massively. Suddenly, I could hear everything, every little sound.

Downstairs, the neighbours had some music on. They

had it really cranked up. They were a Native couple and they were always getting drunk and having these loud parties. Normally, in our bathroom you could make out little bits of muffled conversation coming from the apartment downstairs, especially if the people downstairs were talking loudly or arguing near their bathroom. That's how shitty the insulation in our building was. Now that I was high, I could hear everything that they were saying to each other—even with the music on.

As soon as my hearing intensified, I started to feel extremely paranoid. Being able to hear all these little noises in the apartment—things that I didn't notice normally when I wasn't high, like the sound of Christine rolling over in bed and the bedsprings stretching, or the sound of the refrigerator compressor turning off and on— really started to freak me out. I started to get this vague feeling of paranoia. One minute I'd hear a creaking noise and I'd think someone was lurking somewhere in the apartment. Then I'd hear a car drive down Ottawa Street and I'd think it was the cops, coming to bust me.

These paranoid delusions were all that I was concerned about. Like any other time that I was high on crack, any legitimate worries that I had in my life didn't even enter my mind. It was like they didn't exist. The crack high just blocked them right out. The high was so intense that I was literally just sitting there on the toilet, thinking to myself, *I am so fucking high right now*, and listening to what was going on around me.

While sitting on the toilet, I found myself searching for little crack crumbs suddenly. I always got this strange compulsion to search crumbs whenever I smoked crack. I'd get this feeling that I'd dropped a tiny crumb while I was smoking and that would get me started. It didn't even matter that I still had more crack to smoke. I searched for crumbs regardless.

Because I was on the toilet, my pants were around my ankles. I reached down and started to check my pants for crumbs by running my index finger along the creases in the material. When I didn't find anything, I started to check the floor. We had ceramic tiles in our bathroom. I checked the grout in between the tiles by my feet. I touched something that felt like a crack crumb. I picked it up and looked at it closely, but I couldn't tell if it was crack or not because my vision was so blurry. It was hard to focus properly. I put the crumb onto the end of my stem very carefully—I was feeling jittery and I was afraid that I would drop it—and then I held my lighter to it for a second to see if it would melt.

About ten or fifteen minutes after doing the first blast, the high wore off. I was still paranoid and my hearing was still intensified because I'd done such a big hoot, but I was no longer high out of my mind. I immediately wanted to do another blast and get super high again. The urge to do this was pretty powerful.

Before I did another blast, I grabbed the towel that was hanging from behind the bathroom door and wiped my face with it. Even though I'd only done one blast, it had been such a big one that my forehead was dripping with sweat.

After wiping my face, I put another piece of crack onto the end of my stem, melted it into the screen a bit, and took another hit. Instantly, I was high again, although not as high as I'd gotten off the first blast that I'd done. Even though I'd done another really big one, it didn't get me as high because I'd done it as soon as the first one had worn off. To get as high as I'd gotten off the first blast, I would have had to wait awhile before doing the second one. I could never wait that long, though. I could never resist the urge to do one blast right after another one.

Within forty-five minutes, I was done smoking the forty piece. I got four big blasts out of it. I did each blast about ten or fifteen minutes apart. Most people would probably get about seven or eight blasts out of a forty piece, but I always did really big blasts compared to most people that I'd seen smoke crack in my life. I had no idea how I was able to do such big ones. It was just the way I always did them.

When the dope was gone, I continued searching for crumbs. After doing this for a while, I wiped my ass, got off the toilet, and went into the living room to push my screen. Pushing my screen involved taking something skinny enough to fit into my stem—I used the plastic tube from inside of a pen—and using it to literally push my screen from one end of my stem to the other. Doing this scraped off some of the crack that had coated the inside of my stem while I was smoking.

After I'd pushed my screen once, I tapped the end of my stem onto the coffee table just to make sure that there wasn't any loose crap in there. Then I held a flame to the end of my stem and inhaled. I got one last hoot by doing this.

As soon as the high wore off, I immediately wanted to get more dope. I wanted to keep chasing that first blast that I'd done. Even though it was impossible to get this high again, I still wanted to try. After doing a few blasts in a row, I wasn't thinking too rationally anymore. I was pretty fucked up. I was just thinking about how great that first blast felt and all I wanted to do was re-experience it. I didn't care how much it cost. If there had been three hundred dollars' worth of dope sitting in front of me, on the coffee table, I literally would have sat there all night, doing blast after blast, until it was all gone. The only thing that stopped me from getting more dope was paranoia. I was so fucking paranoid, thinking the cops were outside my apartment, looking for me, that I couldn't bring myself to leave the house.

Seeing as how I couldn't get any more dope, I decided to just call it a night. I put my stem back onto the bathroom shelf, turned off the light, made sure that the front door was locked, and then went to bed.

In the bedroom, Christine was passed out. I got into bed beside her and pulled the blanket over myself even though I was still sweating. I tried to fall asleep, but I was still feeling the effects of the crack I'd smoked. Even though the crack high only lasted for about ten or fifteen minutes, it could take quite a while to fully come down from it. The paranoia and jitteriness, in my experience, could last for up to a couple of hours. Now that I wasn't high out of my mind anymore and I was starting to come down, I started to experience all these horrible thoughts.

You can't keep doing this, I told myself. You swore to yourself before you went to Edmonton that you'd stop smoking this shit all the time and hiding your drug habit from Christine.

These were the types of thoughts that I would think whenever I was coming down off a crack high. I didn't like the fact that I'd been lying to Christine about my drug habit, so whenever I was coming down, that's when I'd beat myself up over it. While I was actually smoking crack, I didn't think about Christine at all. The crack just blocked all that right out. It was only when I started to come down that I started to think about her. The guilt could be really intense. Sometimes I'd literally have to snort a Percocet, or smoke some weed, to take the edge off. I didn't have either thing on me, though. On this particular night, I just had to deal with it.

The thoughts lasted for about an hour. Shortly after that, I fell asleep.

2

I didn't sleep very long that night. After only a few hours, I got woken up to Christine's alarm clock beeping in my ear. I opened my eyes and looked at the time on the clock. It was seven o'clock in the morning.

The alarm clock stopped beeping suddenly. The next thing I knew Christine's hand was on my chest and was reaching down to my cock. Because Christine and I hadn't had sex for three weeks, the minute she touched my cock it got hard as a rock. Christine turned onto her side, stuck out her ass, and in a few minutes, I was already coming.

After we had sex, Christine got out of bed. It was the first day of the winter term at university and she had to get ready for class.

"Honey, can you drive me to school?" Christine said, as she put on her housecoat.

"Sure," I said, even though I was feeling really tired and

would have rather stayed in bed. "What time does your class start?"

"Nine o'clock."

"OK. What time do we have to get out of here by?"

"We should probably leave by about twenty after eight."

Christine went into the bathroom to take a shower. I got out of bed, pulled on a pair of jeans and a sweater, and went outside onto the balcony to have a smoke.

Outside, it was still dark. As I stood under the dim balcony light, I started to think about what I'd done the night before and, immediately, I started to feel bad about it. I'd really thought, while I was in Edmonton, that I'd managed to quit my drug habit. I couldn't believe that within an hour of getting back to Hamilton, I'd used the shit again.

I finished my smoke and went back into the apartment. I made coffee, and then sat down on the couch and drank a cup while Christine got ready for school.

At ten after eight, I went down to warm up the car. About ten minutes later, Christine came down. We got on the road and took King Street to McMaster University, which was in the west end of the city.

When we got the university about twenty-five minutes later, I dropped Christine off in the parking lot off Sterling Street and told her that I'd pick her up later, when she was done school. I didn't usually pick Christine up from school or drop her off in the mornings because I usually worked temp jobs. Since I hadn't gone to work that day, I figured that I might as well pick her up.

"OK, thanks," Christine said. "You can pick me up at five o'clock."

Christine gave me a kiss and then got out of the car.

"Love you," I said.

"Love you, too," Christine said.

I got back on the road and took Main Street home. By the time I got home, the effects of the coffee had worn off and I was feeling tired again. I decided to go back to bed.

I slept until around eleven thirty. As soon as I got up, I had a smoke, and then sat down in the living room to download some movies off a torrent site on my laptop. I hadn't downloaded anything since before I'd left for Edmonton. There were a lot of new releases to catch up on.

I started a bunch of downloads. After that, I had nothing to do. For a second, I thought about going over to my buddy Dave's to kill some time until the movies downloaded. I knew Dave from the carnival. I lived in the building next door to him. Dave hadn't worked since the carnival season had ended in October, so I knew that he'd be home; I just wasn't sure if I felt like dealing with Belinda, Dave's girlfriend. She and I didn't get along.

After thinking about it, I decided not to go over to Dave's. I just wasn't in the mood to deal with Belinda. To pass the time, I decided to watch a movie I'd already seen on my computer. I figured that it would be far more entertaining than anything on TV. We only got two channels that came in clearly on the antenna. There was never anything good to watch on either one of them.

Twenty minutes into the movie, I started to feel bored with it. Suddenly, out of nowhere, I thought about going over to Chester's and getting some dope. I tried really hard to think about something else, but just like the day before, once the thought to get high entered my mind, I couldn't stop thinking about it.

Before the movie was over, I decided that I couldn't take sitting there and thinking about crack anymore. I had to give into the craving or it would never go away. I got up off the couch, threw on my coat, and went down to my car.

Fuck it, I thought, as I drove over to Chester's. Get high one last time and then that'll be it.

When I got to Chester's, it was around one thirty. Chester had gone out somewhere, but Sal and his girlfriend were home. I waited around for about twenty minutes, while Sal and his girlfriend finished smoking the dope that they were smoking, and then went with Sal to a convenience store down the street to meet the dealer. I bought a forty piece, gave Sal a ten-dollar tip, dropped him off, and then went home.

Since I was home by myself, I got high in the living room. Once I was high, I felt so fucking paranoid that I grabbed a screwdriver—to be used as a weapon, if necessary—and then closed all of the doors in the apartment. Any room that I couldn't see inside of from the living room, like the bedroom and bathroom, had to have the door closed. In my fucked up state of mind, I kept thinking that someone was lurking in the apartment, waiting to attack me. My hearing was so intensified that I would hear a noise, turn my head, and I would literally feel the air move, as if someone had just walked past me. If the doors weren't closed, I didn't feel safe.

At one point, some people came in through the street door after I'd just done a really big blast. I immediately thought that it was the cops. I went straight to the front door, made sure that it was locked, and then sat down in the living room, just hoping that the cops wouldn't come upstairs to my apartment. The people walked up the stairs and knocked on the downstairs neighbours' door. I felt so relieved. I immediately got up and made sure that the bedroom and bathroom doors were still closed, and then I checked the front door again.

When I was done getting high, I went into the bedroom to lie down while the effects of the drug wore off. The comedown was terrible, as usual. The whole time that I was coming down, I kept staring up at the crown moulding above the bedroom door and wondering why I seemed to have such little control over my drug use.

That afternoon, at around four thirty, I left the house to pick up Christine. The paranoia and jitteriness that I'd been feeling since getting high were pretty much gone by this point and I was OK to leave the house and drive somewhere.

I got to the university before Christine's class got out. While I waited in the parking lot, I listened to the radio. A few minutes after five o'clock, Christine came out of one of the buildings. She got in the car and we headed home along Main Street.

On the way home, Christine asked me about my day.

"It was OK," I said.

"That's good," Christine said. "What'd you do?"

"Ah, not much. I just hung around the house and watched a couple of movies."

Christine didn't ask me any more questions. She started telling me about her day. I listened to her as much as possible, but my main focus was on the traffic, which was backed up along Main Street, coming over Highway 403.

At Main and Balmoral, which was two blocks west of Ottawa Street, we stopped at the No Frills grocery store. Christine and I hadn't been at the house for a while and we were out of almost everything. We filled the cart up with all the basics—bread, milk, bananas, etc. When we got to the checkout, Christine, as usual, paid with her credit card.

As soon as we got home, Christine put the groceries away and heated up the leftovers that her parents had given us the night before. It had been a few hours since I'd gotten high, which meant that I was starting to get my appetite back. Crack always killed my appetite for quite a while after I smoked it.

We had a pretty quiet evening at home that night. Christine did some studying and then we watched one of the new movies that I'd downloaded.

Later, as we were getting into bed, Christine wanted to know if I was going to go to the temp company in the morning.

"No, I've got some things to do tomorrow," I told her. "I've got to go to the bank in the morning and pay my car insurance. I'm definitely going to go on Wednesday, though. After I pay my insurance, I'm going to be pretty broke."

Since I didn't go to the temp company in the morning, I drove Christine to school and told her that I'd pick her up later, at five o'clock, when she was done. After that, I went straight to the TD bank at Centre Mall to pay my car insurance. The mall was just down the street from our house, on Barton, in between Ottawa and Kenilworth. The mall was in the process of being torn down and redeveloped into a big box complex, but the TD bank was still open. It hadn't been torn down yet. I went in there and paid my insurance, which was about two hundred and fifty dollars.

After paying my insurance I still had a few bucks left, so I stopped at a convenience store and bought a pack of smokes. I wasn't too heavy of a smoker. A pack would last me a couple of days. In the winter I even smoked Viceroys, a cheaper brand of smokes than Du Maurier, which I preferred, to save money. After buying the smokes, I was broke. I literally didn't have a dollar left to my name.

I left the convenience store and went home. I had a bowl of cereal and then sat down on the couch to watch a movie on my laptop. The day before, when I was downloading movies, I'd come across a movie starring Mickey Rourke, called *The Wrestler*. It had just come out before Christmas and I'd managed to get a screener copy.

The movie turned out to be pretty good. It kept me pretty entertained. As I watched it, some of the scenes reminded me of when my parents used to take me and my brother and sister to see Stampede Wrestling matches when we were kids, before their divorce. Stampede Wrestling was really big in Alberta back in the eighties. It was where a lot of guys from the WWF got their start. Stu Hart and the Hart Brothers, Bad News Allen, the Dynamite Kid—they were all Stampede Wrestlers before they made it big. Even though *The Wrestler* was kind of a depressing movie in places, it brought back some good memories.

When the movie ended, I put on another new movie that I'd downloaded. I didn't really feel like sitting and watching another movie, but I had nothing else to do.

The movie turned out to be kind of a B-movie. I wasn't that into it. I put on another movie, but it wasn't much better. Pretty soon, I started to think about getting high again.

Shit, I thought. What the hell else is there to do around here during the day?

I was glad that I'd paid my car insurance that morning because I knew that if I hadn't, I'd be going over to Chester's and buying a forty piece. Since I didn't have any money left, the only thing that I could do to get high was clean out my stem.

The best way to clean out a metal stem was to use rubbing alcohol. We had a bottle of ninety-nine percent isopropyl rubbing alcohol in the bathroom, which was perfect. I went into the bathroom, got the alcohol, and then went into the kitchen and got a plastic Tupperware container and a small ceramic plate.

I went back into the living room with the stuff and sat down on the couch. I picked up my stem, removed the screen, and then cleaned the stem out with the alcohol over the Tupperware container. To do this, I just poured a little bit of alcohol into the stem and then shook the stem in between my thumb and index finger. I did this for about ten seconds and then dumped the liquid into the container. The liquid that came out was a brownish colour. I repeated this process until the alcohol that came out of the stem was clear.

Once I'd cleaned out my stem, I poured some of the alcohol from the container onto the ceramic plate. Then I lit the alcohol on fire. The flame was pretty big, but because I'd only put a small amount of alcohol onto the plate, it wasn't big enough to set off the smoke detector in the apartment. When the flame burned out, I poured some more alcohol onto the plate and lit it on fire. I kept repeating this process until all the alcohol in the container was gone.

When all of the alcohol was gone, and the plate was cool to the touch, I picked up an X-Acto blade and started to scrape off all of the shit that had burned onto the plate. I started at the edge of the plate and worked my way towards the middle. This was the most time-consuming part of the whole process. It took quite a while to scrape all the shit off.

As soon as I was done scraping, I was ready to smoke. I gathered all of the scrapings into a pile, scooped it up with my X-Acto blade, and put it onto the end of my stem. I melted the scrapings into my screen with my lighter and then I did a hoot. It gave me a pretty good buzz.

After cleaning out my stem, the rest of the day just dragged. When it was finally four thirty, I drove to the university and picked up Christine.

The trip home was uneventful at first. When we got to Sherman Avenue, however, something screwy started happening with the car. We stopped at a light. When the light changed, I pressed down on the accelerator. Suddenly, the engine revved high, making the whole car vibrate.

"What was that?" Christine said.

"The transmission," I said.

I didn't know too much about cars, but I knew the basics. We were definitely having some kind of problem with the transmission.

I was afraid that the car was going to break down in the middle of the road, so I turned onto the next street that we came to, pulled over, and turned off the ignition. I waited for about a minute and then turned it back on. The car started up fine.

"Is the car OK?" Christine said.

"I don't know," I said. "We'll find out in a minute."

I had a really bad feeling that the car was going to break down as soon as we got back onto Main Street. We weren't too far from home, though. My objective was to just get the car home.

I got back onto Main and continued heading east, towards Ottawa. I drove a couple more blocks and then we stopped at another light. After a few minutes, the light changed. I pressed down on the accelerator, but the car didn't move this time, the engine just raced.

I immediately knew that the transmission was fucked. I

put the car into park and jumped out of the car. I looked at the ground. Surely enough, transmission fluid was leaking out all over the pavement.

I opened my door to turn on my hazard lights. "The car's fucked," I told Christine.

"What do you mean it's fucked?" Christine said.

"I mean it's done, baby. All the seals just blew on the transmission. There's fluid leaking out all over the place."

I glanced over my shoulder and looked down the street. That part of Main Street was a one-way, four-lane road. There was a break in the traffic, but the cars were catching up to us.

I turned to Christine. "I need you to take the wheel," I said.

It was a simple enough request but Christine looked at me like I'd just asked her to perform open-heart surgery. Unlike most people who grew up in the suburbs, Christine had never learned to drive. She had a driving phobia, she'd told me. She didn't even really like being in a car as a passenger. That's how much anxiety she had.

"Take the wheel?" Christine said. "Jim, do you realize who you're talking to?"

"Yeah, I know," I said. "But we don't have a choice here, Christine. The car's still drivable. We're in the middle of the road."

"But why me?"

"Who else am I going to ask?

"I don't know. Can't you do it?"

"OK. Do you want to get behind this thing and push, then?"

Christine shut her mouth and slid into the driver's seat. She looked up at me as she nervously took hold of the wheel.

"We need to get onto the side street," I said.

At the light we were at, Main Street intersected with a residential street. All Christine had to do was make a right-hand turn at the corner and then pull the car over to the curb.

"Now, the power steering ain't working," I said, "but you'll be able to turn the wheel fairly easily because the car will be in motion."

Christine gripped the steering wheel. "I think I can do this," she said.

I got behind the car and pushed as Christine steered the car onto the side street. She hit the curb a little as she pulled the car over, but she otherwise did all right.

As soon as Christine had the car pulled over, she got out of the car and we called for the tow.

About fifteen minutes later, the tow truck showed up. Christine and I had the car towed to a garage on Main Street that was walking distance to our house. It was the same garage that I'd taken the car to the first time it had broken down. Back in October, about a month after I'd bought the car, I was driving to a temp job one morning when the engine blew.

We got to the garage just before six o'clock. Like most of the small businesses in the area, they were about to close.

"You can leave your car on the street, across from the garage, and come back tomorrow morning," the mechanic told us. "We open at 9 a.m."

Christine didn't have class until eleven o'clock the next day, so we got up in the morning and walked over to the garage.

As soon as we got to the garage, the mechanic hauled the car inside and took a look at it. Then he told us what I already knew. "Your transmission's done," he said. "I won't be able to repair it. You're going to need a new one."

"How much is that going to cost?" I said.

The figure was over a grand.

"Look, man, we just dropped eleven hundred dollars here a few months ago on a new engine," I said. "Can't you give us a deal? It's the only reason we brought the car back here. We could have taken it someplace else."

The mechanic wiped black grease off his hands with a rag. He hesitated for a second. "I can put in a refurbished tranny if you want," he said. "It'll be cheaper. I'll only charge you eight fifty, including labour. The only thing is you won't get your car back until Monday. I've got to order the part. It'll take a few days for it to come in. I won't be able to start working on it until the weekend."

I looked at Christine, since she'd be the one paying for the repair.

"Refurbished is fine," Christine said.

The three of us went into the mechanic's office. The mechanic sat down at his desk and drew up the bill of sale. I hung back, by the door, as Christine paid with her credit card.

We left the garage and walked to the bus stop on Main Street. It was almost ten o'clock and Christine had to get to class.

Christine didn't say much to me as we stood there, waiting for the bus. I could tell by her body language, though, that she was pissed. She was obviously pissed that the car had broken down again, but I think that she was also pissed at herself for having dumped more money into fixing it. Christine kept grumbling to herself and checking her watch every few seconds, like she was annoyed with the bus or something, but it didn't take a genius to figure out what was really going on inside her head.

After waiting for what seemed like forever, the bus finally showed up. Christine got on it and I headed home.

As I walked back to the apartment, I started to think about how boring the rest of the week was going to be, now that I was going to be stuck at home until Monday with no money and nothing to do to pass the time. Without a car there was no point in even going to the temp company. The temp company that I'd been going to before my trip to Edmonton handed out work assignments on a first come, first served basis. All the guys who went there regularly took the bus, so if you didn't get there before the busses started running in the morning there was no guarantee that you'd get an assignment. There were other temp companies in Hamilton, but they never seemed to have consistent work available. If Christine was going to lend me bus fare, I wanted to at least make sure that I was going to get some actual work.

When I got to our building, I started to feel pretty depressed. I went upstairs to the apartment and took a nap for a while . . .

3

Two days after the car broke down, Christine took the GO Bus to Toronto to her second job as a casual at the public library. She worked there two days a week, on Thursdays and Fridays, shelving books.

With the weekend looming, I decided to call my ex-girlfriend Nicole. I wanted to let her know that, due to my car being broken, I wouldn't be coming by on Friday night to pick up Emily.

As soon as the words were out of my mouth, Nicole freaked out on me. "What do you mean, you won't be picking her up?" she said. "You told me that you'd take her this weekend, Jim. I already made plans."

I didn't know what the hell kind of plans Nicole could have made that she couldn't have broken or rescheduled. She didn't work; she was a welfare case who just sat on her ass all day. I didn't want to argue with her, though.

"Look, I know that I promised to take her this weekend, Nicole, but my car just broke down," I said. "I won't be able to get to Toronto."

"Why don't you just come here on the GO Bus and pick her up, then?" Nicole said. "You used to do it all the time before you got your car."

"Yeah, I know, but I don't have any money right now; that's the thing. With my car being broken, I wasn't able to get any temp work this week."

In the background, I heard the sound of a young kid screaming suddenly. It was Nicole's other kid—the one that she'd had with the guy she'd left me for. The screaming was ear piercing. I had to pull the phone away from my ear for a second.

Nicole said something to her dickhead boyfriend and then got back on the phone. "Jim, I've got to go," she said. "My kid's screaming."

"Yeah, no kidding," I said.

"Call me when your car's fixed, OK?"

"OK, bye."

It took me a few minutes to calm down after talking with Nicole. Even though the conversation had only been about thirty seconds, it managed to get me pretty worked up. I hated Nicole so much that it was hard to even have a short conversation with her. Just the sound of her voice irritated me. I'd done the right thing by calling her, but in a way, I wish I hadn't bothered.

Why give that bitch advance notice? I thought. You should have just called her on Friday night at six o'clock to tell her that you wouldn't be coming.

By the time Friday night rolled around, I was feeling pretty bored and depressed. I was out of cigarettes, so I was also extremely crabby. I decided to call my mom in

Edmonton to see if she'd send me a few bucks. I was hoping that she'd send me enough to get a couple packs of smokes and maybe a quarter ounce of weed.

My mom wasn't too thrilled that I was calling her, asking for money. "Send you money?" she said. "I just spent a fortune to fly you and your daughter out here for Christmas, Jim. What happened to the money that I gave you before you flew back to Toronto?"

"I put it all on my car insurance," I said.

This was a lie, of course. I'd spent a hundred dollars' of it on crack.

"Didn't you get any temp work this week?" my mom said.

"No, I couldn't get there," I said. "My car broke down again."

I could tell that my mom felt bad for me that my car had broken down again, but she still wouldn't give me any money.

"Look, I'm sorry, son, but I just can't help you right now," my mom said. "Your stepfather and I spent a lot of money over Christmas. We're really trying to watch our spending. You'll just have to wait until your car's fixed and you can get to the temp company."

I talked to my mom for a few more minutes, just so she wouldn't think that the only reason I'd called her was to ask her for money. When we were done talking, I hung up the phone and tossed it onto the couch.

For a while, I moped around the apartment. Christine got tired of my bad mood, finally, and offered to give me money to buy a pack of smokes.

"You don't have to do that," I told her.

"Yes, I do," Christine said. She took two five-dollar bills out of her purse and handed them to me. "Here," she said.

"Now please go to the store and get some cigarettes."

I reluctantly took the money and then went out and bought a pack of smokes. Shortly after I got home, my buddy Dave came over. Dave was a huge pothead. He brought a joint over, which was a huge relief.

Christine didn't smoke weed, so Dave and I smoked the joint together. While we smoked, Dave told me about his Christmas with Belinda, which hadn't been too eventful. I told him about my trip to Edmonton, and then about how my car had broken down.

When I was done telling Dave about my car, I asked him if he wanted a coffee. We were done smoking the joint now and we were just hanging out.

"No, thanks," Dave said. "I've got to get going."

"Why?" I said. "You just got here."

"I know, but I've got a poker tournament starting soon."

Dave was really into online poker. He played for hours every day on his laptop. Sometimes he played with real money, but he mostly just played the free tournaments.

"OK," I said, rolling my eyes. "Go home, then, Dave. Go play your tournament."

I got up and followed Dave to the kitchen to see him out.

As Dave was heading out the door, he turned to me suddenly in the stairwell. "Hey, I wanted to ask you," he said in a really quiet voice. "Could you get me some Percs, man?"

This was obviously the real reason that Dave had come over: to ask me if I could get him some Percocet. Dave didn't do Percocet, but his girlfriend Belinda did sometimes. She complained that she had back pain from a car accident years ago. I knew a guy in Hamilton who sold his prescription, so I'd do Dave a favour and get him some pills once in a while.

"Sure," I said.

Dave gave me a hundred dollars.

"I'll get them on Monday, as soon as I get my car back," I said, as I put the money into my pocket.

"Thanks," Dave said.

"No problem."

On Monday morning, at around nine o'clock, the garage called to tell me that my car was finally fixed. Christine had already left for school. I hung up the phone and immediately walked over to the garage to get my car.

When I got to the garage, the mechanic wanted to talk to me for a few minutes. He wanted to give me some advice on maintenance.

"When was the last time that you had your oil changed?" the mechanic asked me.

"I don't know," I said. "I haven't done it yet."

"How long have you had this car?"

"Since September 2008."

"Well, you should get it changed soon. I looked at it while I was working on your car and it's really dirty. I also noticed that your brake pads are getting thin—the front ones, especially. You should consider getting them replaced."

Sure, why don't I just give you some more money? I thought. Christine had just dropped eight fifty on a transmission and here this guy was, trying to hustle more out of us.

"As soon as I get a few bucks together, I'll get some work done this car," I told the mechanic.

"OK, but I wouldn't wait too long," the mechanic said. "You don't want to wait until your brake pads are so thin that you're grinding your rotors. I'll give you a deal if you let me do the work."

I got into my car and got the hell out of there before the mechanic could point out anything else in my car that needed maintenance. Then I drove to my pill guy's house and bought Dave the Percocet he'd asked for. I got a hundred pills for a hundred dollars and kept fifty pills for myself, charging Dave two bucks a pill. That was the deal. I didn't use Percs that much, but I did use them once in a while, like whenever my ankle was bothering me—I'd sprained it by jumping out of my game one summer and it still hurt from time to time—or when I was coming down from a crack high and wanted to take the edge off.

After leaving my pill guy's house, I went over to Dave's. Dave was in the middle of a poker tournament, so I didn't stay long. I gave him the pills, smoked a joint with him, and then I went home.

4

The day after getting my car back, I went to the temp company that I'd been going to before my trip to Edmonton. The temp company was in the east end of Hamilton, off Barton and Centennial, which was about a ten- to fifteen-minute drive from our house. The place didn't open until six thirty in the morning, but I made sure to get there at five, before the people who took the bus there started to show up. I parked in my usual spot, right in front of the temp company door, turned off my ignition, and then sat in my car under a blanket.

A few minutes before six thirty, I got out of my car and walked up to the temp company. There were a bunch of guys standing outside the door by this time, waiting to get in. I took my place at the front of the line. All the guys that were there were regulars. They all recognized me and knew that I was there first, so no one gave me any shit.

As soon as I got inside the temp company, I walked up to the counter. The broad who'd opened the door to let us all in was a different broad than the one who'd been working there before my trip. I introduced myself to her and she pulled up my file in the computer system.

"OK," the broad said, after looking at my file for a few seconds. "Please wait a moment, sir. We'll be assigning jobs to people shortly."

I took a step back from the counter, feeling kind of confused. I couldn't understand why the broad hadn't just given me a work assignment. I couldn't understand why I was being told to wait.

I glanced over my shoulder and was surprised to see that no one was standing behind me. Usually, everyone lined up to get a job from Sandy, the broad who usually worked behind the counter. Instead of being in a line, the guys were all standing around by the entrance. By the way that they stood, you couldn't even tell who'd gotten to the temp company before whom.

I walked over to where all the guys were standing. After waiting around for a few minutes, the broad behind the counter glanced down at a clipboard and then looked up at the crowd, above her reading glasses.

The room fell silent.

"Mr. McDermott?" the broad said.

One of the guys walked past me and went up to the counter. The broad handed him a card. This was the card that told you where you had to go, what time you had to be there—that sort of thing.

As soon as buddy took the card, he turned and walked out the door.

The broad called out another name. "Mr. Boland?" she said.

I felt someone trying to move past me. I stepped aside and watched another guy walk up to the counter. The broad gave him a card, and then he left, too.

"The rest of you, please come back tomorrow," the broad said. "That's all the work assignments we have for today."

A bunch of grumbling erupted from the crowd of guys standing by the door. The guys turned and left, but I just stood there, not being able to move.

After a few seconds, I kind of snapped out of it. I walked back up to the counter. "Uh, excuse me," I said.

"Yes," the broad said. "How can I help you?"

"I thought jobs were assigned here on a first come, first served basis. How come those two guys got work? I was here way before them. I was first in line."

"I'm sorry, sir, but we select people for jobs here based on how well-suited they are for the job, not based on the order in which they arrive here in the morning."

"Well, I was coming here all the time back in the fall and that isn't the way you guys operated. Is this a new policy or something?"

"I'm not sure. I just started here."

"OK, fine. What if I just wait around here, then? If something comes up later this morning that I'm suited for, could you send me to the job? I can get there right away. I've got a car."

"We don't usually get calls for same-day work assignments past 6:30 a.m.—at least not since I've been here. It's better if you come back tomorrow morning."

"Why? So you can pick and choose who you send out again?"

"Like I said, sir, that's our policy."

I hated myself for sounding desperate, but I had no choice but to beg to this broad. "Please," I said. "I'm really hurting right now. I just need a few hours' work. Is there any way that you could just put my name down on the list for tomorrow? I've got a lot of work experience. I can do any job."

The broad wouldn't budge. "Sir, I'm really sorry, but there's nothing that I can do for you," she said. "I can't go against company policy. You'll just have to come back tomorrow morning. If we get an assignment, and we feel that you're the person who's best suited for it, we'll give it you."

My heart sank. I shrunk away from the counter. "Ah, blow me," I muttered. Then I turned and walked out the door.

I left the temp company and drove straight home. When I got home, Christine had just gotten up and was getting ready for school.

Christine was pretty surprised to see me. "I thought that you were going to go to the temp company this morning," she said.

"I did go there," I said.

"What happened?"

"I couldn't get any work. I don't think that I'll be able to get any work there anymore. They're picking and choosing who they're giving work assignments to now for some reason."

Christine noticed how depressed I looked. She asked me if I was OK.

"Yeah, I'm fine," I said. "Don't worry about it. You've got to get ready for school now. You know how long you take. I'll drive you, OK?"

I sat down on the couch while Christine got ready for school. When she was ready to leave, we went down to the car and I drove her to the university.

After I'd dropped Christine off, I decided to stop by some of the other temp companies that I knew of in Hamilton. As it turned out, none of them had any work. I filled out their paperwork, even though I knew that the chances were slim that any of them would ever call me. Then I went home feeling even more depressed.

I had nothing to do to pass the time when I got home, so I put on a movie that I'd downloaded. It was a really bad cam. The audio was OK, but the picture was total crap. I watched it for a while and then fell asleep.

A couple of hours later, I woke up from my nap. I downloaded some more movies and smoked a couple of butts, since I was out of cigarettes again.

As I sat down to watch another movie, I started to feel so fucking sorry for myself. All I could think about was how horrible things had been going for me since getting back from Edmonton and how many more months I had to get through until the carnival season started and I was working again. The carnival season usually started in about mid-April. I had a lot of time left to kill.

At around four thirty that day, I left the house to pick up Christine. I thought that seeing Christine would cheer me up, but Christine had had a bad day too from what I could tell. As soon as she got into the car, she started bitching to me about this statistics course that she had to take for her Master's degree in sociology.

By the time we got home, the conversation had somehow shifted to what had happened to me earlier that day at the temp company. Suddenly, Christine wasn't bitching to me anymore about her stats course. She was bitching *at* me, and asking me what my plans were for finding work.

What the hell did I do to deserve this? I thought.

I really wasn't in the mood to talk about work right at

that moment. I'd just suffered through rush hour traffic and was dying for a smoke. It was bad enough that I was out of smokes and had to smoke butts. I just wanted to be left alone.

"How about we talk about this tomorrow?" I said, as I sat down on the couch. "I haven't really thought about what I'm going to do yet."

"Did you think about maybe trying some other temp companies?" Christine said.

"Yeah, I already did that."

"When?"

"This morning, right after I dropped you off."

"Oh, yeah? What happened?"

"None of them had any work available."

"Why don't you just look for a regular job, then, honey? Even if it's only part-time, you'll probably get more hours than you were getting at that temp company in the fall. It didn't seem like they ever had much work there."

I'd actually gotten a lot of work at the temp company. Every day that I'd gone there, I'd gotten a full day's work. The reason Christine thought that I hadn't gotten much work there was because I'd lied to her about how many hours I'd been getting in order to hide my drug habit from her. At the time, I was smoking a forty piece after work every day. If Christine had known how many hours I'd really been getting, she would have wondered, after a while, why I was always too broke to help out with the bills.

In terms of getting a regular job, Christine knew that there wasn't much available to me. I'd never finished high school. I only had my Grade 10.

"What kind of job do you want me to look for?" I said.

"I don't know," Christine said. "What about pizza

delivery, or something? You don't need a high school diploma to do that, and you already have a car."

I didn't really like the idea. I was thirty-three years old. Delivering pizzas seemed kind of demeaning to me. It was something that my own dad had done, the odd time that he'd actually worked while I was growing up. My dad had only managed to get a Grade 6 education. He used to joke all the time about how he'd walked into the front doors of the junior high school and then walked right out the back. Delivering pizzas was basically the only kind of job that he could get.

Even though I disliked the idea, I told Christine that I'd think about it. I thought that Christine would start making supper and leave me alone, but she didn't. She kept badgering me about finding work. She was apparently tired of me not making a financial contribution to the relationship and wanted things to change.

"When I moved in with you in September, you told me that we'd be splitting all of the household bills fifty-fifty, remember?" Christine said. "Since your season ended after Thanksgiving, though, I've been paying for everything. I know that you weren't getting too many hours at that temp company that you were going to in the fall, and I knew that you had to pay car insurance and have some money to see your daughter on the weekends, which is why I didn't bug you about it, but I really need you to start helping me out with the bills, Jim. That car repair really set us back. You're going to have to start looking for a job now, OK?"

"OK," I said. "I'll look."

Christine must have felt that she'd made her point because she immediately stopped bothering me and went into the kitchen to make supper.

As soon as Christine was out of the living room, I

grabbed a butt from my ashtray on the coffee table and headed for the door.

In the kitchen, Christine had just taken some hot dogs out of the freezer. "How many do you want?" she asked me. "One or two?"

I looked at the food and felt sick. "None," I said.

Christine looked at me with concern. "What do you mean, 'none'?" she said. "You're not going to eat supper?"

I realized the nerve this struck with Christine. This was the same kind of crap I'd pulled almost every single night from the time the carnival season had ended in October, when I'd started working temp jobs and smoking crack every day after work, until I'd left for Edmonton in December. After finishing work every day at around three o'clock in the afternoon, I would cash my paycheque, get a forty piece of crack, and then go home and get high. By the time Christine came home later and made supper, I wasn't hungry yet and didn't want to eat anything. Christine had no idea why I never wanted to eat supper, or when I did eat, why I ate so little. We got into arguments over it.

Seeing how irritated Christine was, I decided to change my answer. "On second thought," I said, "why don't you make me two hot dogs, baby? I'll eat one now and have the other one later."

Christine nodded, but she looked skeptical, as if she didn't really believe that I would actually eat the two hot dogs. I watched her break off a couple of hot dogs and plunk them into a pot.

I went outside onto the balcony and had my smoke. It was nice out there. It was quiet. It had just started to snow and the air was really still.

As I stood out there, smoking and watching the snow fall down from the sky, I started to think about how I was going to find a job, given how shitty the economy was. It was 2009 and a lot of people were getting laid off. It wasn't just happening in Hamilton, with the steel industry, it was happening everywhere. Now that I couldn't get any temp work in Hamilton, I didn't know where to look for work. Without a high school diploma, I didn't have too many options. A lot of places wouldn't hire you anymore if you didn't have your Grade 12.

I thought about other types of jobs that I might be able to do with my level of education and the fact that I also had a criminal record, which didn't help, but no ideas came to me.

Pizza delivery, I thought. Yeah, that's about all you're qualified to do.

The thought depressed me tremendously. Suddenly, I wasn't thinking about finding work anymore, I was just thinking about getting high. Even though I didn't want to smoke crack anymore, I knew that after one blast, I wouldn't be thinking about my problems. There was no other way to get that kind of relief from the stress that I was feeling.

If Christine hadn't already bitched at me to look for a job, I might have just gone back into the apartment and asked her if she could lend me some money. Seeing how irritated Christine already was with me, I knew that that wasn't an option. It would have only resulted in an argument, which I didn't need. Dave was the only other person that I could ask for money, since I had no other friends in Hamilton. But he was as broke as I was and he had just spent a hundred dollars on pills for Belinda.

Fuck it, I thought. It's hopeless.

Just as I was ready to give up and go back inside the apartment, I looked at the dark, snowy sky and suddenly I thought about Chester. My very next thought was of his roommate, Sal.

Sal was a typical crackhead in the sense that he was always broke and trying to hustle up money for dope. Sometimes when I went to Chester's and Sal was around, he'd try to reel me in to do one of his stupid scams with him. I always turned Sal down because I always had money when I went there—either from the show, if it was during the carnival season, or from the temp company, if it was during the winter. On this particular day, though, I was feeling really desperate.

Sure, Sal's scams might be stupid and risky, I thought, but what are the chances we'll actually get caught?

Not having any better ideas, I went back inside the apartment and told Christine that I was going to go out for a while.

"What do you mean, you're going out?" Christine said. "I'm making supper. We're about to eat."

"I know, but I think that I should go see my friend," I said.

"Who? Dave?"

"No, this guy from the temp company. I was talking to him this morning, when I went there. He told me that he's got a snowplow. He gave me his address and told me to drop by if starts to snow. It just started snowing right now, while I was out there, smoking. If it keeps up, I might be able to get some work with this guy tonight, plowing driveways. I'd be nice to make a few bucks, don't you think?"

It was a pretty good story, given the weather.

Christine bought my story, but she didn't want me to rush out of the house so quickly. "Are you sure that you don't want to eat your hot dog first?" she said. "It'll be ready in a few minutes. If you're going to go out and work, honey, you should at least have something to eat first."

"I'll eat when I get back," I said. "I want to get over there right away. I don't have this guy's phone number. I want to get over there before he leaves the house."

Christine stopped pushing me to eat supper. She must have realized that she wasn't going to get anywhere with me on that issue. After bugging me all fall about it with little to no success, I think that it finally sunk in.

I gave Christine a kiss. "I'm not sure when I'm going to get home, but I'll call you if I'm going to be really late," I said.

"OK," Christine said. "I love you. Drive safe."

5

There were a bunch of people smoking crack at Chester's when I got there that night. Luckily, Sal was around. I pulled him aside, bummed a smoke off him, and then asked him straight-up if he had any scams.

"You know I've got scams, Jim," Sal said. "What are you in the mood for?"

"I don't know," I said. "Think of something, man. You've got a driver."

Christine had told me to make use of my car when she'd suggested that I get a job doing pizza delivery. This wasn't exactly what she'd meant, but at least I'd be putting my car to some use, I figured.

"All right," Sal said. "I've got a couple of ideas. Just let me finish my beer, OK?"

I waited for Sal to finish his beer. When he was done, he tossed the empty beer can into the pile of trash by the coffee table, went to the bathroom to take a piss, and then we left the apartment.

Outside, it was still snowing. We got into my car and drove to a house not far from Chester's. I waited in the car while Sal went inside.

A few minutes later, Sal came back to the car. He had a disappointed look on his face.

"What happened?" I said.

"Ah, there's nothing going on here," Sal said.

"Well, that was fun."

"Don't worry, Jim. I've got another idea."

We got back on the road and Sal had me take him to this other place. It was in the same general area as the first house we'd gone to. Just like at the first house, however, there was nothing going on.

"I can't believe it," I said. "The one time that I actually want to do a scam with you, Sal, there's nothing going on."

"Relax," Sal said. "Let's just drive around for a while. I'll think of something."

For almost an hour I drove Sal around, as it continued to snow. Finally, he got an idea.

"Hey, I know what we can do," Sal said.

"What?" I said.

"We can rip off a newspaper box."

The idea was so fucking random. Who the hell ripped off a newspaper box? I wondered.

"Uh, I don't know, man," I said. "Do you really think there's that much money in one of those things?"

"Sure there is," Sal said. "A buddy of mine ripped one off one time when he was jonesing. He scored about eighty or ninety bucks, he told me."

Since neither of us had any better ideas, we decided to do it. We needed some bolt cutters, though, first, since newspaper boxes were usually chained up. Sal had some bolt cutters at home, so we stopped by Chester's, Sal got his bolt cutters, and then we got back on the road.

We drove around for a while, but we had a hard time finding a newspaper box that we could rip off. The only ones that we found were on the main drags, where they were too much in plain sight.

"How the hell did your buddy rip one of these things off?" I asked Sal. "These things are all in really conspicuous areas."

"I don't know," Sal said. "I never asked him."

"Well, what do you want to do? Do you want to try to come up with another idea?"

"No, let's keep looking. There's got to be one around here somewhere."

We drove around for another half hour, but we still couldn't find anything. It hadn't stopped snowing yet and the roads were starting to get pretty bad.

"You know what we should do?" Sal said.

"What?" I said.

"We should head up to the industrial area."

The industrial area was in the north end of Hamilton, around Burlington Street. It's where the steel mills and the manufacturing companies were located.

"What the hell do you want to go up there for?" I said.

"At this time of night, there shouldn't be too many people around," Sal said. "There might be some newspaper boxes up there. People go to work and want to grab a paper, you know? I think we should check it out."

Just when I thought that things couldn't get any worse, I found myself driving around the industrial area with Sal, hunting a newspaper box to rip off. It was truly the end of the line. I'd wasted my time, gas, and patience, and I still didn't have what I wanted. I was almost ready to tell Sal to forget it, when suddenly, there it was.

"See," Sal said. "What'd I tell you?"

We were somewhere around the old Stelco plant, driving down a deserted, snow-covered street that ran in between two factories. Up the street, at the intersection, was a stop sign. Lo and behold, chained to it was a newspaper box.

"Here's good," Sal said.

"Here?" I said.

"Yeah, pull over."

We were about twenty feet away from the newspaper box, but Sal was already starting to open his door.

I stopped the car. Sal got out and quickly took off down the street, leaving a trail of footprints behind him in the snow.

When Sal got to the stop sign, he took a moment to peer around. Then he stepped into the snow bank and cut the chain attaching the newspaper box to the stop sign with his bolt cutters.

After Sal cut the chain, he looked around again and then quickly walked back to the car. "Let's make a U-ey here and go back the way we came," he said. "We'll drive around for a while, just in case someone was watching us. Then we'll come back for it."

I turned the car around and we took off down the street. Twenty minutes later, we came back for the newspaper box.

"Try to get as close to it as you can," Sal said.

I pulled the car over as much as I could.

"All right, that's pretty good," Sal said.

Sal and I got out of the car. I went around to Sal's side of the car, opened the back passenger door, and then walked over to the newspaper box.

Sal had pulled a pair of work gloves out of his pocket and was putting them on. "Make sure to lift with your knees, OK?" he told me.

"Sal, don't tell me how to lift," I said. "I know what I'm doing."

Sal brushed the snow off the top of the newspaper box and then began to tilt the box towards him. I squatted down to the ground. I didn't have any gloves on me, so I had to pull the sleeves of my coat down over my hands. It didn't give me much grip, but it was better than my hands getting stuck to the fucking thing.

Sal and I lifted the newspaper box and walked it over to the car. I ended up having to get into the backseat with it and literally walk it through to the other side.

"Do you have any extra room at your end?" Sal asked me when it was time to close the doors.

"No, I'm right up to the edge," I said.

"OK, let's try to close these doors, then. It's going to be a tight fit."

The newspaper box was so long that we almost couldn't close the doors. We had to push all of our weight against the doors as we were closing them, just so they'd close properly.

Once the newspaper box was in the car, and the doors were shut, we took the blanket that I kept in the car for those mornings at the temp company and draped it over the newspaper box. Then we drove back to Chester's.

In behind Chester's building was an area large enough to park a couple of cars. We parked back there and then took the newspaper box out of the backseat and set it down on the pavement.

"What now?" I said.

"Let's take it down to the basement," Sal said.

The basement in Chester's building was directly beneath Chester's apartment. You went in through a door on the side of the building and you could go either to Chester's apartment or down to the basement. Chester was the only person in the building who had access to it.

Sal and I picked up the newspaper box. We brought it around to the side of the building, maneuvered it through the door, and then took it down to the basement. It was a bitch from hell getting it down there. The staircase was this rickety old thing. A few steps were loose and wobbly, probably from the wood being rotten. It was damp down there and it smelled like mould.

As soon as we got the newspaper box into the basement, Sal checked out the lock on it. The lock jutted out from the side of the box and was surrounded by a piece of metal. There was a little hole in the metal where the newspaper guy would stick the key in to get at the coin box. I knew the kind of lock it was. It was unpickable.

"Well, there's no way we're going to get that fucking thing off," Sal said. "I'm going to go upstairs and ask Chester if we can use his grinder."

Sal went upstairs to the apartment. A few minutes later, he came back down the stairs with Chester. In Sal's hand was Chester's grinder. It was one of those hand-held multi tools with a grinder as one of the attachments.

As soon as Sal and Chester got down to the basement, Sal started to look for a place to plug in the grinder. He looked around for a couple of minutes, but he couldn't seem to find a place to plug it in.

"What's the matter?" Chester said. "You need your glasses or something?"

"No," Sal said.

"What's the problem, then?"

"I don't think there's any electrical outlets down here!"

Chester nearly died laughing. "You guys probably should have looked into that before hauling this thing all the way down here," he said. "What does this thing weigh, anyway? It looks like it weighs a fucking ton."

Sal swore at Chester under his breath. He booted the newspaper box, spun around, and then started pacing.

I decided that it was time to leave. "Well, that was a waste of time," I said. "All right, Sal. I'm out of here."

I started to head for the stairs.

"Wait," Sal said. "I've got an idea."

"What?" I said.

"We could get an extension cord and run it up the stairs to the apartment."

Chester laughed again. "Sal, just up those stairs, there, is about ten or twelve feet," he said. "You got an extension cord that'll reach that far? You know, sometimes I think that when they were handing out brains, you thought they said 'pains,' so you told them that you didn't want one."

"I've got a fifty-foot extension cord at home," I said. "I can go home and get it if you want. It'll only take a second."

"Would you, Jim?" Sal said.

I headed up the stairs, as Chester and Sal continued bickering. When I got home a few minutes later, Christine was sitting in the living room, studying.

Christine put her book down and came to greet me at the door. "Hey, honey," she said. "How'd it go?"

"All right," I said. "I managed to get some work. I'm not done yet. I just came home for a second to get something. Buddy's waiting for me downstairs in his truck."

I quickly wiped off my shoes and then went into the bedroom to get the extension cord. The cord was something I'd bought the summer right after my ex-girlfriend Nicole had left me, when I was living in a bunkhouse on the show with Dave. They'd had a sale at Canadian Tire one day on extension cords. Dave and I each bought a fifty-footer with the built-in locking mechanism, connected the two cords, and then ran it to the show's generator so that we could have power all the time in our bunkhouse for our laptops.

I found the cord in a banana box at the bottom of the closet. I untangled it and went back to the kitchen with it.

"What's with the cord?" Christine said.

I knew that there would be questions as soon as Christine saw the bright orange extension cord, so I already had a story figured out.

"I'm helping someone move," I said.

"Move?" Christine said. "I thought that you were doing snow removal."

"I was, but then the guy's friend called and said that he needed help moving out of his apartment."

"What do you need an extension cord for?"

"We need more light at the back of the truck. The guy's friend has a cord, but it ain't long enough."

Christine seemed satisfied with this explanation. "OK," she said. "What time do you think you're going to be home tonight?"

"I'm not sure," I said. "I'll probably be home within a couple of hours. This guy doesn't have a lot of stuff. The move's been going really fast."

"All right, honey. See you soon."

I drove back to Chester's and went down to the basement. Sal and Chester were still bickering. I handed Sal the extension cord. Sal immediately plugged the cord into the grinder, ran the cord up the stairs to the apartment, and then came back down to the basement.

The lock was so tough to cut through that it took Sal forty-five minutes and five zip disks to get the goddamn thing off. Luckily, we were directly beneath Chester's apartment and the walls of the basement were solid concrete. Had Chester's neighbours been able to hear us, they might have wondered what the hell we were doing, running a grinder down there for forty-five minutes, and called the cops.

Once Sal got the lock off, he opened the newspaper box and grabbed the coin box. He immediately shook it, looking to see how many loonies he could spot. "Let's go upstairs and count this shit," he said.

The people who'd been smoking crack at Chester's earlier that night were gone now. The place was empty. We needed a place to count the change, so Chester swept some of the trash that was on the coffee table onto the floor and then Sal dumped the change onto the table.

We crowded around the coffee table and counted up the money. By the time that we were done, there were stacks of nickels, dimes, quarters, and loonies all over the table. It only amounted to forty-seven dollars, though.

"I can't believe it," I said. "Only forty-seven bucks."

"Let's count it again," Sal said. "I think I might have made a mistake."

I could feel a horrible throbbing pain in my forehead. It was getting greater by the second. "We already counted it," I said. "I ain't fucking counting it again, Sal. There's forty-seven dollars in that fucking thing, not a penny more!"

I hung my arm over the side of the couch and felt a crusted stain brush up against my hand. It could have been a cum stain for all I knew, but I didn't even care. We'd spent all that time and energy, and had taken all that risk, and we didn't even have enough for a fifty piece. And that had to be split three ways, since we'd used Chester's grinder and probably twenty dollars' worth of his zip disks. Then there was the added headache of having to give all that loose change to some crack dealer somewhere. Not that that would be a problem. Most crack dealers would accept any little money you had. But it was the pain in the ass of having to wait for the dealer, only to get about fifteen dollars' worth each.

I looked over at Sal again, re-counting the change. "Hey, quit counting that shit and get a jar, or a bag or something already," I said. "I want to go meet this guy so I can go home."

Sal got a shopping bag and put the change into it. We drove to a convenience store on Barton Street and met the dealer. The dealer took the change and gave us our piece. I drove Chester and Sal home and we each took our cut. Then I drove home and got high in the bathroom, while Christine sat in the living room, studying.

6

The day after stealing the newspaper box, I woke up in the morning and drove Christine to the university for eleven o'clock. On our way over there, I realized that I was running low on gas. I had pretty good gas mileage on my car, a 1999 Chevy Malibu, but I hadn't filled up for a while, and after driving Sal around the night before, I was almost on empty.

"Hey, baby, I need to fill up," I said to Christine.

"OK," Christine said. "Let's stop at the Petro-Can."

Up the street, at King and Sherman, was a Petro-Canada gas station. We stopped there and filled up.

Even though I'd supposedly worked the night before, plowing driveways and doing a moving job, when we went inside to go pay, it was understood that Christine would pay for the gas. Anytime that I was driving Christine anywhere and we needed to fill up, she always put the gas on her credit card. It had been like that ever since I'd bought my car. I think that because I'd bought the car and because I was paying for the insurance every month, Christine felt that it was only fair to fill me up when I was driving her somewhere.

The gas came to about forty dollars. Before Christine paid, I asked her if she'd throw in a pack of smokes. I didn't really want to ask her, but I was jonesing so bad. I was expecting Christine to say no, but she agreed without hesitation. She was obviously in some kind of generous mood. Christine was a pretty moody person, though, so this wasn't that odd.

We got back on the road and I dropped Christine off at the university. After that, I went to look for a job. I was determined to get working again and to start helping Christine out with the bills. Since Christine had suggested pizza delivery, I decided to start with that. Even though the idea of delivering pizzas didn't really appeal to me, at least it was a paycheque, and at least it would include tips, I figured.

For a few hours, I drove around lower Hamilton, looking for pizza joints. I hit up a whole bunch of them, but as it turned out, none of them were currently hiring drivers. A couple of places gave me their application and encouraged me to fill it out in case a position became available in the future.

I drove home with the full intention of filling out the applications and bringing them back later, on my way to pick up Christine from school. When I got home, however, I started to feel pessimistic. Suddenly, the thought of applying for jobs that didn't currently exist—or which might never exist anytime in the near future—seemed pointless to me. I put the applications down on the coffee table and told myself that I'd fill them out later if I changed my mind.

To pass the time, I put on a movie that I'd downloaded. About an hour into it, my phone started to ring.

I grabbed my phone from off the coffee table.

Ugh, I thought, as I looked at the caller ID. It was my ex-girlfriend Nicole.

The reason Nicole was calling was because she wanted to know if my car was fixed yet.

"Yeah, it's fixed," I said.

"Oh, good," Nicole said. "You'll be picking up Emily on Friday, then?"

"No, I can't this week."

Nicole let out an exasperated sigh. "What do you mean, you can't, Jim?" she said. "Why not?"

"Because I'm broke," I said. "I haven't been able to get any temp work yet. I don't have the money to make two roundtrips to Toronto to pick up Emily and bring her back."

"What about Christine?"

"What about her?"

"Didn't you tell me once that she works in Toronto on Fridays?"

"Yeah, so?"

"So, why can't she pick up Emily on Friday after she finishes work? That way, you only have to worry about bringing her back on Sunday. I'm sure that you can afford that."

I knew that Nicole didn't really care if Emily saw me or not. She just wanted to get rid of her on the weekends.

"Why don't you leave Christine out of this?" I said. "This ain't her responsibility."

"Why don't you step up, then, and start acting like a dad

to your kid?" Nicole said. "This is two weeks in a row now that you're not going to see her, Jim."

Before the argument could get any more heated, I told Nicole that I had to go. "I'll see Emily when I've got some money," I said.

"When's that going to be?" Nicole said.

"I don't know. I'll call you."

"Yeah, like you called me to tell me that your car was fixed?"

"Sorry, but I've really got to go, Nicole. My other line's ringing."

I ended the call and put the phone down on the coffee table. I was so pissed off that the first thing I wanted to do was get high. I'd only smoked about fifteen dollars' worth the night before, though, which for me, wasn't even two big hoots, so there was no point in even cleaning out my stem.

For a second, I thought about going over to Chester's to see if Sal was around. I was thinking of doing another scam with him. That's when it suddenly occurred to me:

Why do some stupid scam with Sal, when the scam might not even work out in the end? Wouldn't it be easier to just drive around an actual crack dealer and have the guy pay you in crack?

It was kind of a crazy idea, but it seemed less and less crazy the more that I thought about it. Driving a crack dealer wasn't any riskier, really, than doing a scam with Sal. As long as the dealer kept his drugs on his person, and didn't put them down in my car, I knew that the cops couldn't charge me with anything if we ever got stopped. Chester knew a lot of crack dealers. I was sure that one of them would appreciate having a driver for a few hours. And at least in the end, I'd know that the crack dealer would actually have what I wanted. I wouldn't be going home with a lousy fifteen dollars' worth of crack.

It didn't take much more convincing for me than that. I immediately threw on my coat, went down to my car, and headed over to Chester's.

When I got over to Chester's house, Chester was in a really bad mood. As soon as he let me in the door, the first thing he did was get on my case about the newspaper box.

"Oh, great," Chester said to Sal, who was sitting down on the couch. "Jim's here. Maybe the two of you can go downstairs now and get that newspaper box shit out of my basement."

I had no intention of moving the newspaper box anywhere. It had been hard enough getting the damn thing down to the basement. As far as I was concerned, if Chester wanted it out of there, that was his problem.

"Sorry, man, but I didn't come here to do a moving job," I said. "I just came here to ask you for a favour."

"A *favour*?" Chester said.

"Yeah, I wanted to know if you could get me in touch with one of your dealers. I want you to hook me up with someone who needs a driver."

Chester looked like he wanted to tell me to go fuck myself. He didn't, though. He knew that he was going to get a tip from the dealer later if he hooked the guy up with a driver and he didn't want to miss out on the opportunity.

After a short trip to the bathroom, Chester sat down on the couch and called up some of the crack dealers that he knew.

"Hey, what's your phone number?" Chester said to me while he was on the phone with one of the dealers.

I gave Chester my number. Chester gave it to the dealer and then hung up the phone.

"So, what happened?" I said. "What's the score?"

"He's interested," Chester said. "He just doesn't need you to drive him anywhere right now. He said that he'll call you later. His name's Bruce, by the way."

"All right," I said.

Later that day, at around twenty after five, Bruce called me. I was in the car with Christine, driving down Main Street on our way home from the university.

"Chester gave me your number today," Bruce told me. "He said that you're looking for someone who needs a driver tonight."

"That's right," I said. "Do you want me to pick you up?"

"Yeah, that'd be great."

Bruce told me where he wanted me to pick him up. It was some bar downtown, on King Street.

"OK, I'm in the car right now," I said. "I'm just on my way home to drop off my girlfriend. I'll be there in about fifteen minutes. I'm in a maroon Chevy Malibu."

"OK," Bruce said. "I'll wait for you out front. I'm wearing a black North Face jacket."

Christine looked at me as I hung up the phone. "Who was that?" she said.

"Oh, just this guy that I met last night while I was moving buddy out of his apartment," I said. "He wants me to drive him around tonight to help him run a few errands. He said that he'll put some gas in my car and pay me a couple of bucks for my time. He wants me to pick him up right now."

"Why does he need you to help him run errands?"

I thought of something quick. "He's old," I said. "He can't drive and he's got a bum leg."

In a few minutes, we were home. I let Christine off in front of our building and then drove downtown to pick up Bruce.

Bruce was standing outside the bar, having a smoke when I got there. He was a middle-aged Chinese guy.

As soon as I pulled up, Bruce looked over at me, tossed his cigarette, and then got into the car.

We immediately worked out the deal.

"I want ten dollars an hour," I said. "You've got to pay me in crack, though, OK? I don't want cash. And don't give me my piece until we're done and I drop you off. I don't want any drugs in my car unless they're on your person."

"All right," Bruce said.

"So, where are we going?"

"The McDonald's across the street from Gage Park."

Gage Park was a big park in central Hamilton. Christine and I passed by it every day when I drove her home from school along Main Street.

I got onto Main Street and started heading east, towards the McDonald's. Suddenly, Bruce's phone started to ring. Bruce reached into his pocket, looked at the number, but decided not to answer it. He just looked at the caller ID and let it ring, which I found pretty annoying.

"Are you going to get that?" I said.

Bruce ended the call and put the phone back in his pocket. "Nope," he said. "He knows I'm coming. He's just going to have to fucking wait."

In about ten minutes, we were at the McDonald's. Bruce's customer was in the parking lot, waiting for us. I recognized the guy. He was someone that I'd seen hanging out once or twice at Chester's.

The customer got into the backseat of my car, behind Bruce. Bruce turned in his seat and handed the customer the dope.

While the customer was still in the car, Bruce took a big chunk of crack out of his pocket and broke off a little piece of it. Then, without even saying anything to me, he pulled a stem out of his jacket pocket and did a hoot right there in the car. In my rearview mirror, I saw that Bruce's customer was doing the same thing, in the backseat.

At first, I was just stunned. I wanted to throw both their asses out of my car and take off, but I was speechless. I kept looking over my shoulder, feeling totally paranoid. Luckily, there weren't any cops around.

A few minutes later, I heard the sound of the back door opening. Bruce's customer got out and quickly took off down Main Street. I got back on the road and said nothing. I reminded myself of the piece that I was going to get a few hours later, when I dropped Bruce off, and managed to keep my mouth shut.

I drove Bruce around and he made some more deliveries. On the way to each one, Bruce got the dope ready in the car, as I was driving. He didn't use a scale to weigh each piece; he just broke off a little chunk, eyed it for a second, and then wrapped it up in a piece of plastic that he tore off of a shopping bag that he had with him.

After Bruce finished making his deliveries, he told me that he wanted to make a stop.

"OK," I said. "Where do you want to go?"

Bruce gave me the address. It was on Cannon Street, not far from where Christine and I lived.

I drove Bruce to the place on Cannon.

"You can come inside, if you want," Bruce said, as he got out of the car.

"How long are you going to be?" I said.

"I don't know . . . ten or fifteen minutes, maybe."

"It's OK. I'll wait in the car."

Bruce went into the apartment. I waited for about twenty minutes, but Bruce didn't come back to the car. I got tired of waiting for him, so I went into my phone's call history, found Bruce's number, added it to my contact list, and then called it. The phone rang a few times and then went to voicemail.

What the hell's going on? I wondered.

I got out of my car, went to the apartment that Bruce had gone to, and knocked on the door. Some guy answered.

"I'm here to get Bruce," I said.

"Oh, yeah?" the guy said. "And who are you?"

"I'm his driver."

"Oh, OK."

The guy let me into the apartment. The place was filthy. It was a total crack house. As soon as I walked in the door, the stench of the place hit me like a wall.

I walked into the living room and found Bruce. He was sitting on the couch, smoking crack with some people.

Bruce looked up at me as I walked into the room. "Oh, hey, Jim," he said.

"What the hell?" I said. "Why wouldn't you answer your phone?"

"Sorry, I must have had the volume turned down."

"Whatever. How much longer do you plan on hanging out here?"

"Why? How long has it been?"

"It's been twenty minutes already."

"OK. Just hold on a second."

Bruce didn't get up, though. He just sat there and did another blast. It took me almost twenty minutes before I finally got him out of the apartment.

Bruce did some more deliveries. Then he told me that he wanted to make another stop.

"Let me guess, another crack house?" I said.

"Why don't you just come inside this time, instead of waiting in the car?" Bruce said.

"No thanks. I don't like hanging out in those places, man. How long are you going to be this time?"

"If I'm not out in fifteen minutes, come get me."

"OK, fine. If I have to come in there and get you, though, you better be ready to leave. The agreement was that I drive you around tonight. I never said that I'd hang out with you in crack houses and watch you smoke crack all night."

I took Bruce where he wanted to go. Just like at the first place we'd stopped at, I had a hard time getting him out of there.

This kind of crap with Bruce went on for the next several hours. By around ten thirty, I was getting pretty tired of it. Bruce and I were at yet another crack house. I was trying to get him out of there, but, as usual, all he wanted to do was sit there and get high.

Suddenly, Bruce's phone started to ring. Bruce answered it, mumbled something into it, and then tossed it onto the seat next to him.

"Who was that?" I said.

"That guy near Stadium Mall," Bruce said. "He keeps fucking calling."

About an hour earlier, we'd met a guy at a convenience store on the corner of Barton and Gage, near Stadium Mall. Bruce had sold the guy a twenty piece, even though he was a couple bucks short. I wondered what the guy had done to come up with more money so fast.

Maybe he knocked someone over the head for it, walking down Barton Street, I thought.

"Bruce, come on," I said.

"Yeah, yeah, hold on," Bruce said.

Finally, I'd had enough. "I'm going to go wait in the car now, OK?" I said. "You'd better be out of here in five minutes."

I went back to my car. A few minutes later, Bruce came out of the house.

Just as we were leaving the parking lot, Bruce felt like being an even bigger pain in my ass.

"Let's stop at a 7-Eleven," Bruce said.

"Why?" I said.

"I want to get a Slurpee."

"Bruce, this guy's waiting for you. Let's just go meet him already."

"So? I don't give a shit about that. I'm thirsty. I need a drink."

There was a 7-Eleven on Main Street, near Sherman Avenue. We weren't too far away from it. I drove Bruce over there so he could get his drink.

As Bruce was getting out of the car to go into the store, he decided, for some reason, to leave his coat behind, in the passenger seat.

"Hey, what are you doing?" I said.

"What?" Bruce said.

"Where's your stuff? Is it on you?"

Bruce paused for a second. He looked at me like he didn't know what the hell I was talking about. "Oh, the *stuff*," he said. "No, it's in my coat."

I picked up Bruce's coat and tossed it to him. "Then put your coat on," I said. "I don't want you leaving your shit in my car."

Bruce angrily shoved his arm into the sleeve of his coat. "What the hell is your problem?" he said. "You're so fucking paranoid. I'm just going into the store for a minute. It's not like there's cops around."

"Just keep your shit on you," I said. "Don't make me tell you again."

Bruce went into the store and came out a minute later with his Slurpee. We got back on the road and drove to Barton and Gage.

When we got to the convenience store, Bruce's customer got into the car and handed Bruce a sandwich baggie full of change.

"There's five bucks in there," the customer said.

Bruce gave the customer five bucks' worth of crack. We got back on the road and Bruce did his last two deliveries.

"OK, I'm done," Bruce said. "You can drop me off at home."

Bruce gave me his address. It was a high-rise off Barton and Centennial, not far from where I used to go to the temp company.

I drove over to Bruce's place. Right before Bruce got out of the car, he gave me my piece. The piece was so small that I had to do a double-take.

"What the hell is this?" I said.

"What do you mean?" Bruce said.

"This ain't even a forty piece!"

"Well, you weren't driving me around the whole time. We made a lot of stops."

"Yeah, and whose fault was that? Anyway, it doesn't matter. You were paying me for my time, man, not just to drive you around. My fee is ten dollars an hour. I told you that when I picked you up at the bar. Now, quit fucking around already and pay me."

Bruce reached into his pocket, but then hesitated.

"What the hell are you waiting for?" I said. "Pay me!"

Bruce broke off another piece of crack and handed it to me.

"Good," I said. "We're done here now. You can get out."

Bruce got out of the car.

I got back on the road and headed straight home . . .

7

I didn't plan on ever dealing with Bruce again after driving him around that night. At ten thirty the next morning, however, guess who called? I was still in bed, after having dropped Christine off downtown that morning to catch the GO Bus to get to her job in Toronto at the library. I felt groggy and tired, but I answered the phone.

"Bruce," I said. "What the hell do you want?"

"I need you to drive me somewhere," Bruce said.

Even though I knew that driving Bruce again was a bad idea, I was unable to turn him down. Driving Bruce meant an opportunity for me to get high. Once Bruce had me on the phone, talking to him, all I wanted to do suddenly was rush out the door and drive him.

"OK," I said. "I'll drive you. But only if you agree to pay me properly."

"Did I not pay you properly last night?" Bruce said.

"You know what I mean, man. I don't want to have to fucking haggle with you about it. You've got to pay me ten dollars an hour. Even if you make a stop, the clock is still running, you got it?"

"Yeah, I got it."

"OK. Where are you?"

"I'm at home."

I told Bruce that I'd be right over and then threw on some clothes and went down to my car.

When I got over to Bruce's apartment, Bruce was waiting for me in the lobby. He got into the car and had me drive him to a drug treatment facility in downtown Hamilton.

"What do you need to go here for?" I said.

"I'm on the methadone program," Bruce said. "I've got to go here every morning."

"What are you, a heroin addict or something?"

"No, I got busted with some pills. It's a condition of my probation."

I honestly wasn't that shocked to hear this. From what I already knew about Bruce, it was hard to imagine him doing any kind of drug treatment without being forced to by the courts.

I let Bruce off in front of the clinic and then found a parking spot on the street, around the corner.

About twenty minutes later, Bruce called me. I drove to the clinic and picked him up.

"I need you to take me to my dealer's house now," Bruce said. "I need to pick up a quarter ounce."

"OK," I said. "Where does he live?"

Bruce told me where his dealer lived. The place was only a few minutes away from the clinic.

I drove to Bruce's dealer's house. Bruce went inside, picked up the dope, and then came back to the car.

Bruce had a few deliveries that he had to make right away, so he did those, and then he had me take him to a crack house. It was the exact same bullshit as the night before. It took me nearly half an hour to get Bruce out of the place.

We drove around some more and Bruce made some more deliveries. At around a quarter to three, I wanted to take a break.

"OK, time to pay me," I told Bruce. "I want to go home now and get high."

"If you want to smoke, why don't we just stop somewhere?" Bruce said. "I know a place nearby."

"I already told you," I said. "I don't like hanging out in those fucking places, man."

"OK, OK."

I got off the road and pulled into a convenience store parking lot.

Bruce reached into his pocket and pulled out the big chunk of crack that he carried around.

"It's been four hours," I said. "You owe me a forty piece."

"Yeah, I know," Bruce said.

Bruce broke off a forty piece and handed it to me. He gave me a pretty good count.

"Call me as soon as you're done smoking," Bruce said.

"OK, I will," I said.

I drove straight home and got high in the living room. By around five o'clock I was straight enough to leave the house.

I called up Bruce. "Hey, I'm done," I said. "Do you want me to pick you up?"

"Sure," Bruce said. "I'm at that bar downtown, on King Street. The one you picked me up at yesterday."

"All right," I said. "I'll be there in a few minutes."

Christine hadn't gotten home from work yet, so as I left the house, I sent her a text:

Hey baby I'm going out to drive that old guy again.
See you tonight. Love you mwa mwa mwa.

I picked up Bruce and drove him around for a few more hours. Then I went home to take another break.

When I got home, Christine was in the living room, studying. She got up and came to greet me at the door.

"Hey, honey, how'd it go?" Christine said.

"It was all right," I said.

"Are you hungry? I can heat up some leftovers in the microwave for you, if you want."

I hadn't eaten anything all day, but I wasn't hungry. I just wanted to get high.

"No thanks," I said. "I already ate."

"Oh, OK," Christine said. "What'd you have?"

"I had some stir fry at buddy's house," I said. "His wife made it. It was really good. They're Vietnamese or something."

Christine went back to her studying. I went into the bathroom. As soon as I got in there, I opened the window a crack, put the bathmat up against the bottom of the door, grabbed my stem from off the bathroom shelf, took a shit, and then got high.

For once, the neighbours didn't have their music blasting. While I sat on the toilet, stoned out of my mind, I listened to Christine, typing away on her laptop. Even though she was about ten feet away from me, and was on the other side of a door, it sounded so loud that it felt like she was pounding the keys right next to my head.

I sat in the bathroom and did another hoot. A few

minutes later, I heard the sound of couch springs stretching and Christine's footsteps coming towards the bathroom door. There was a pause and then a knock.

"Jim?" Christine said.

Christine's voice gave me a nervous jolt. I knew that I had to answer, but I was so stoned that I was afraid to speak.

"Yeah?" I said, finally. "What is it?"

"Are you all right in there, honey?" Christine said.

"Yeah, baby, I've just got the shits again."

The night before, after I'd come home from driving Bruce and had gotten high in the bathroom, I'd told Christine that I'd had the shits. This wasn't really true, of course. I'd had a little bit of diarrhea right before I'd smoked, but after that, I was fine. I just figured that having the runs was a good excuse to be holed up in the bathroom.

Outside the bathroom door, Christine was quiet for a second. The floor creaked as she shifted her weight to her other hip.

"Can I come in?" Christine said.

If my heart hadn't already been beating like a drum, it would have been.

"OK, hold on," I said, as I tried to stall for time.

I jumped up and immediately stashed my dope and my stem. Then I pulled the bathmat away from the door, sat back down on the toilet, gave the toilet a flush, and sprayed some air freshener.

Christine came into the bathroom. As soon as she got inside, she wrinkled her nose and glanced around the room.

Right away, I thought that I was busted.

"What's that smell?" Christine said. "Were you burning matches in here or something?"

Huh? I thought. Matches?

I really couldn't understand Christine's reaction. Christine had been in a room with me a couple of times when I was smoking crack, back when we first got together, before I told her that I would stop smoking it. She knew what the shit smelled like. She'd seen me high. Why she couldn't identify it now was beyond me.

I decided to just go along with the way that Christine was reading the situation. "Yeah, my lighter died," I said. "Sorry, baby. I just had a couple of puffs."

"That's OK," Christine said. "I don't mind if you smoke in the bathroom when you're not feeling well, honey."

Christine reached her hand out and touched my forehead. "You feel warm," she said. "And sweaty. Do you want me to get you some Tylenol? I think you've got a fever."

"No, I'll be fine," I said.

I was hoping that Christine would leave it at that and just leave the bathroom. But she didn't. She kept standing there, talking to me. It made me feel extremely paranoid. It also really killed my buzz.

"Well, how about I get you something to drink, then?" Christine said. "You should drink lots of fluids when you have diarrhea. You don't want to get dehydrated."

I looked up at Christine. As soon as our eyes met, my eyes darted away from hers. It might have made me look guilty, but I couldn't help it. I was so high. It was hard to focus my eyes on anything for more than a few seconds.

"OK, you can get me a drink," I said.

"Do you want juice or pop?" Christine said.

"Juice is fine."

Christine left the bathroom. A few minutes later she came back with a tall glass of purple juice.

"Sorry it took so long," Christine said. "There was no juice made in the fridge. I had to make it from the can. It was frozen solid."

"That's OK," I said.

Christine handed me the glass of juice. My hand was shaking a bit as I took the glass from her, but I tried not to draw attention to it. I casually brought the glass to my lips and took a sip, which was hard to do without spilling any because my jaw felt so tense.

I put the glass down on the ledge of the bathtub.

"Feel better?" Christine said.

"Yeah," I said. "I needed that, baby. Thanks."

I sat there on the toilet for what seemed like forever, waiting for Christine to leave. Finally, she did.

"Let me know if you need anything else, OK?" Christine said to me on her way out the door. "I've got to get back to work now. I've got a lot of reading to do tonight."

Christine went back to her studying and I went back to my smoking. I did another blast, pushed my screen, and then I was done.

I opened the door and came out of the bathroom.

Christine was sitting on the couch, reading. She looked up at me. "How are you feeling?" she said.

"Better," I said. "I think that my stomach's starting to settle down."

I went into the bedroom and lied down on the bed. I closed my eyes for a few minutes and tried to relax, but I was coming down now and all those horrible thoughts were swirling around in my head. I took a deep breath and tried to think about something else, but the thoughts in my head wouldn't stop. A car with a loud muffler came roaring down Ottawa Street, right below our bedroom window. The sound made me jump.

Just then, my phone started to ring. I got out of bed, went into the living room, and picked up the phone. It was Bruce.

"Hey, are you done?" Bruce said. "I need you to pick me up."

"No, not yet," I said. "Give me another half hour."

In half an hour I knew that I would still be feeling a little paranoid, but I'd be straight enough to leave the house.

I hung up the phone.

"Who was that?" Christine said.

"That was buddy," I said.

"The guy you're driving?"

"Yeah."

"What did he want?"

"He wants me to drive him across town."

"Jim, you're not feeling well. You should have told him that you can't drive him."

The negative thoughts in my head were so intense at that moment that, as insane as it sounds, I actually wanted to tell Christine the truth. I wanted to tell her about my drug use and about how I'd been driving around a crack dealer.

Without even hesitating, I reached into my pocket and pulled out a baggie. It was a little drug baggie that I'd had a couple of Percocet in. I always kept a couple on me, in case my ankle was bothering me. I'd done the last one that morning and still had the baggie in my pocket.

I showed Christine the empty baggie. The Percocet had rubbed against the plastic, making it look like there had been some kind of white powder inside of it.

"The guy that I've been driving left this in my car tonight," I said. "I found it after I dropped him off."

Christine took a closer look at the baggie. "What is that?" she said.

"I don't know," I said. "It looks like he had some kind of powder in here."

"What kind of powder?"

"I'm not sure. Cocaine, probably. Either that, or heroin."

Christine had a horrified look on her face. "Jim, what are you trying to say?" she said. "Are trying to tell me that you think this guy's a drug dealer?"

"Yeah," I said. "It would definitely explain why he wants me to drive him around all the time. I don't know where he goes or what he does when I drop him off, but I don't think that he's really running errands. I think that he's having me take him to his drug deals."

My intention in telling Christine all of this was to make it easier for me to tell her the truth about my drug use. If Christine thought that I was being honest with her about the guy that I was driving, the moment that I became suspicious of him, I figured that she would be more sympathetic towards me when I told her why I'd agreed to drive the guy in the first place—to support the drug habit that I'd been hiding from her, and which I'd been struggling to quit.

When the moment came to tell Christine the truth, however, I just couldn't get the words out of my mouth. I was afraid that Christine would leave me and go back home to her parents, or that I would ruin her term at school. It didn't help that Christine was already freaking out about the guy being a possible drug dealer.

"I don't think that you should drive this guy anymore, Jim," Christine said. "You should call him up right now and tell him that you can't drive him."

I immediately regretted the decision to tell Christine anything. Seeing as how I'd already opened my mouth, though, I had no choice but to do damage control.

"You know, now that I think about it, Christine, that baggie might have just had some pills in it or something," I said. "I doubt the guy's a drug dealer. He probably just carries some pills on him for his own personal use."

Christine wasn't convinced. "You don't know that for a fact, Jim," she said. "What if he really is a drug dealer? I mean, think about it? What the hell kinds of errands could he possibly have to do right now, at this time of night? It's after nine o'clock. All the stores are closed."

It was a pretty good point. I thought of something quick. "He told me that he wanted me to drive him across town to his daughter's house," I said. "It sounds plausible. That might be where he's really going."

"I still don't think that you should drive this guy," Christine said. "If he is a drug dealer, you're taking a big risk. What if you get pulled over by the cops and they find this guy in your car? He might be known to the cops in Hamilton. How are you going to explain what you're doing with him, Jim? You've got prior drug convictions."

These "prior convictions" were from some marijuana charges that I'd gotten in Toronto in the late nineties, and which I'd done jail time for.

"Baby, those charges are old," I said. "No cop is going to care about some old pot charges. Anyway, I already did time for them. I've got no outstanding warrants. If the cops were to run me in their system, nothing would happen. I don't even have any unpaid parking tickets."

"What about the baggie you found?"

"What about it?"

"If the cops found that in your car, couldn't they arrest you?"

"No. The baggie is empty. The cops wouldn't get too far with that. It only has trace amounts of drugs in it. That's probably why the guy left it in my car. I don't think he would have left a baggie in my car if it had actual drugs in it."

"Well, what if they search the guy that you're driving?"

"Then they search him. If he's got drugs on him, then they bust his ass and take him to jail. Nothing would happen to me in that situation. I wouldn't have any drugs on me. There wouldn't be any drugs in my car. I would just tell the cops that I don't know the guy that well; that I'm just giving him a ride somewhere. The cops can't arrest me for just giving some guy a ride. How am I supposed to know where he goes or what he does when I drop him off?"

"I still think it's a bad idea."

"Yeah, but it's a little bit of money right now, Christine. I'll just keep my eyes open when I'm around this guy, all right? I'll make sure that he doesn't leave anything in my car, like baggies, even if they're empty. That way, there's absolutely no risk."

I knew that Christine was still nervous about the idea, but she had to trust me. Between the two of us, I was the only one who really knew about the criminal justice system and how it worked. I hadn't just read about it in some sociology book, I'd actually been involved with it in real life. I knew what the cops could do if they stopped you. I knew what they could charge you with and what they couldn't. Christine didn't have a clue about any of that shit.

"I guess you're right," Christine said. "I'm probably just being paranoid."

"You are," I said. "Trust me. It'll be fine."

Christine went back to her studying. Half an hour later, I'd come down enough and was straight enough to leave the house.

As I walked down the stairs to my car, I thought about

how close I'd come to telling Christine the truth and was glad that I hadn't.

You might be able to tell her at some point in the future, I told myself, once you've kicked this drug habit and this is all ancient history, but you definitely cannot tell her now.

8

I drove Bruce around for a few more days and then decided one morning that I wasn't going to drive him that day; that I wasn't going to get high. It wasn't just the lying to Christine that was bothering me, it was my drug use. I was using way too much, I felt. Before my trip to Edmonton, I was doing forty dollars' worth every day after work. Once I started driving Bruce, I was doing about eighty to ninety bucks' worth every day that I drove him, besides the first night, obviously.

Even though I really wanted to quit smoking crack, when Bruce called me up later that morning, asking me to take him to the methadone clinic, I immediately agreed to do it. Once the opportunity to get high presented itself, I just couldn't seem to turn it down.

While I was worried about my drug use, Christine started to worry about my health. As far as she knew, every night, for four or five nights, I'd had the runs.

"You should go see a doctor, honey," Christine told me one night after I'd finished smoking crack in the bathroom. "You've been getting diarrhea a lot over the last several days."

The last thing I wanted to do was go see a doctor. This wasn't because I knew that nothing was wrong with me; it was because if I went to see one, and the doctor did a piss test, and if he tested for drugs, I was afraid that the doctor would say something to me about all the crack that was in my system while Christine and I were in his office. Crack only stayed in your system for three days. I was doing it every day, though, so I knew that I would never piss clean.

"OK," I told Christine. "If I'm still having these symptoms in a few more days, I'll go see a doctor."

I had no intention of seeing a doctor, though.

To get Christine off my back about seeing a doctor, I started telling her some nights that I was constipated. It was just as valid an excuse to sit on the toilet and it seemed to make Christine feel better that I wasn't shitting my guts out every night.

After a few days of this new cover story, Christine went out and bought me some Metamucil. She prepared a glass of it and handed it to me one night, hoping that it would help relieve my constipation.

I took the glass, but I didn't take one sip of it. I didn't pour it down the sink or anything, I just didn't drink it. Christine never handed me another glass of Metamucil after that, so she obviously got the hint.

Once I started to drive Bruce around every day, the days started to roll by pretty quickly. Before I knew it, it was the end of January. I still hadn't paid my phone bill yet, which had been due earlier in the month, so after being able to only receive calls for nine or ten days, the phone company cut my phone off.

Christine and I didn't have a home phone in our apartment. We both just had our cell phones. Without a working phone, I had no way of contacting Bruce.

I asked Christine if she'd let me use her cell phone for a while, just until I was able to pay my bill. At first, Christine said no.

"Please," I said. "I have no way of keeping in touch with the old guy I'm driving. How will he be able to call me when he wants me to pick him up?"

"OK, fine," Christine said. "Just be careful not to use too many minutes. I don't get too many a month. I have to share them with my sister."

Christine had a cell phone under her parents' plan. They had a family plan and Christine and her younger sister, who was an undergraduate student at the University of Waterloo, shared the talk time. Each month, Christine's parents paid both kids' phone bills.

"Don't worry," I told Christine. "I'll be careful not to use too many minutes."

"There's another thing, too," Christine said.

"What?"

"I don't want you to give my phone number to your ex."

Christine couldn't stand my ex-girlfriend Nicole. Nicole had been rude to Christine a couple of times, at the beginning of our relationship, and after that, Christine refused to have anything to do with her. If I had to pick up Emily, for example, I went to Nicole's house by myself. I understood how Christine felt about Nicole having her phone number—she didn't want Nicole to be contacting her. Nevertheless, I thought that she was being unreasonable.

"Christine, I've got a kid," I said. "What if Nicole needs to get a hold of me?"

"Tell her to use MSN or Facebook," Christine said. "You said that her sister's got an internet connection, right? Anyway, what's the big deal? You're not even seeing your kid right now. Why would she need to get a hold of you?"

"What if there's an emergency? What if something happens to Emily all of a sudden and she needs to get a hold of me right away?"

"I don't know, Jim. It's not my responsibility to make sure that you have a working phone number that your ex-girlfriend can reach you at. I'm sure that if there was a real emergency, Nicole would call your mother in Edmonton and your mother would let you know right away."

That was pretty much the end of the conversation. Sometimes there was just no use in arguing with Christine.

"OK," I said. "I won't give her your number, if that's how you feel."

"Good," Christine said.

Christine handed me her phone. I immediately went into another room with it and called up Bruce. Bruce had been trying to get a hold of me for a while and was wondering what was going on.

"Every time I call you, it says that your number is unavailable," Bruce said.

"Yeah, I know," I said. "My phone just got cut off. You've got to call me on this line now. The calls have to be really short, though, OK? It's my girlfriend's phone. She doesn't want me using up all of her minutes."

If my phone getting cut off wasn't bad enough, that same week, we had problems again with the car. I was driving Christine downtown to catch the GO Bus to get to her job in Toronto at the library, when, suddenly, the car broke down on us. It was the transmission again. The one we'd just put in.

It was so cold that morning that we had to wait inside of a Tim Hortons for the tow truck to show up. Christine decided to call in sick at the library and come with me to the garage.

When we got to the garage, the mechanic was in as much shock as we were. "Wow, I can't believe it," he said. "The part must have been faulty."

"You think?" I said. "It's only been a couple of weeks."

"Don't worry. The part is still under warrantee. I'll only charge you for the labour."

Christine agreed to pay for the repair job without getting into an argument with me. I guess that she was thinking the same thing that I was thinking:

What the hell else can happen to this car before the season starts and I'm working again on the show?

The mechanic had to order the part, just like the last time the car had broken down. As soon as Christine and I got home, I called Bruce to tell him that I wouldn't be able to drive him around for a few days.

"When do you think you'll get your car back?" Bruce said.

"Sometime early next week," I said. "The mechanic's got to order the part."

"OK, whatever. Just call me as soon as you get it back."

That weekend the temperature stayed extremely cold. The daytime highs were in the minus teens. Our landlords, an Indian couple named Rajeev and Harriet, didn't have the heat turned up high enough in our apartment. It got so cold in there that Christine and I would make a cup of coffee and in five minutes, not only the coffee but the cup itself would be cold to the touch. Christine had to put little gloves on to type on her laptop. She kept sniffling and blowing her nose. We had to turn the stove on every so often and stand in front of it, with the stove door open, to warm ourselves up.

I might have been better able to deal with this situation had I not been jonesing to smoke crack. I was, though—badly. It made me feel extremely irritable and unable to concentrate on anything for more than a few minutes. It also made me fart a lot more than usual. Now that I wasn't smoking crack all day, I actually had an appetite. I was starting to eat actual meals again, rather than just little bits of food here and there, enough to get me by. The sudden change in my eating habits was a shock to my stomach. Christine didn't know what was wrong with me. "God, this is bad even for you!" she'd say whenever I'd let one rip.

Throughout the weekend I kept calling the landlords to ask them to turn up the heat, but they didn't respond. By Sunday night, I finally couldn't take the cold in the apartment anymore. I left the landlords a nasty voicemail message, threatening to report them to the Landlord and Tenant Board if they didn't turn the heat up, but even that didn't generate a response.

At around midnight that night, Christine and I went to bed. We had to huddle together under the blanket with our clothes on to keep warm. I wasn't farting so much by this point, so it was actually possible for Christine to be under the blanket with me.

"That's it," I said, as we were lying there in the darkness, shivering. "First thing tomorrow, I'm calling the Landlord and Tenant Board on these assholes."

In the morning Christine got up and took the bus to the university. Right after she left, I looked up the number for the Landlord and Tenant Board on the internet and called it. I spoke to some broad. After explaining the situation to her, she told me that an inspector would be coming over soon.

Within the hour, the inspector showed up. The guy had a digital thermostat and some other gear with him. He checked the temperature in all of the rooms in our apartment. The readings that he got were below twenty degrees Celsius, which violated the by-law in Hamilton.

"What happens now?" I said. "Are you going to call my landlord?"

"I'll do that, but first I've got to check the temperatures in the rest of the units in this building," he said. "There were a couple of reports made for this address today."

Shortly after the inspector left, the landlords came by and turned the heat up in the building. It just so happened to be the second of February, which was the first business day of the month, so they also came around to collect the rent cheques.

Christine had left the rent cheque for me on the light switch by the door. I gave the cheque to the Harriet.

"How's the temperature in here now, Jim?" Harriet said.

Harriet was acting so sweet and nice to me now, after ignoring my phone calls all weekend, it was disgusting.

"Better," I said. "It was about seventeen degrees in the bedroom when the inspector was here."

Rajeev came into the apartment. He touched one of the walls in the living room. "The reason it gets so cold in here is because there's so little insulation in these walls," he said. "Feel how cold this wall is."

I touched the wall. It was cold.

"This place was built in the twenties and it wasn't kept up," Rajeev said. "There's probably almost no insulation in these walls anymore."

I knew that what Rajeev was saying was true, but it wasn't just the insulation in the walls that needed replacing. The whole building was falling apart. As soon as you walked into the stairwell, you smelled rotting wood.

Rajeev went back into the kitchen. He touched the radiator by the door. "When it gets cold in here, you need to bleed these radiators," he told me.

I watched Rajeev as he reached his hand around the radiator and loosened the little cap. A low hissing sound escaped from it.

"You need to do that every so often," Rajeev said. "That lets the air out so that the water inside can circulate."

"OK," I said. "I'll be sure to do that."

I knew that my heating problems didn't have much to do with loosening little caps on radiators, though. The landlords had had the heat down so low that bleeding the radiators wouldn't have made much of a difference.

While I still had the landlords in my apartment, I decided to crack to them about my floor, which was peeling off in the kitchen. I peeled back a piece of linoleum by the fridge with my foot to help demonstrate how bad the situation was.

Harriet caught a glimpse of the brown, dried-up glue on the floor, underneath the linoleum. She sighed deeply, as if trying to convey to me that she actually gave a shit. "I know that your floors are bad, Jim, but we're really short on funding right now," she said. "We really can't afford to replace your floor."

What a crock of shit, I thought.

The landlords had just renovated one of the vacant units in the building, which a previous tenant had trashed. They obviously were more concerned with fixing up that unit, so that they could cram another tenant in there and start collecting some rent, than with fixing my floor.

The landlords left my apartment and then went to collect the rent from the Native couple who lived downstairs. I stood outside on my balcony, having a smoke, as I watched them go down the stairs to the Natives' apartment. When they got to the landing, Harriet knocked on the neighbours' door. No one answered. She knocked again, but there was still no answer.

Harriet and Rajeev came back up the stairs.

"I guess they're not home," Harriet said.

"Oh, trust me, they're home," I said. "They're pretending that they ain't home because they know that it's rent day, and they know that you'll be coming around to ask them for money. It's the only day out of the entire month that those people are actually quiet."

Harriet looked a little bit hurt by the remark. Or maybe she was just stressed out from all the Tenant Board bullshit.

"Thanks for letting us know about your neighbours, Jim," Harriet said. "I'll definitely say something to them about the noise."

I took the last puff of my smoke, put it out, and then went inside my apartment.

Yeah, somehow I doubt that, I thought.

9

The day after the landlords dropped by, I got my car back. I drove Bruce around that night, and then, in the morning, I got up and drove Christine to school. It was a Wednesday. Christine had her stats class. She was really worried about her midterm that was coming up at the end of February.

"I'm really struggling with this course," Christine told me on our way to the university. "I don't know what I'm going to do."

"You worry too much," I said. "I bet you'll do fine."

"What are you basing that on, Jim?"

I didn't have much of a response. I had seen Christine struggling with her stats. Every week she had an assignment to complete, and every week she had to pull an all-nighter just to finish it.

"I screwed up my last two assignments," Christine said.

"I don't even know what the hell is going on in this course anymore. Maybe if I had more time to study, I'd be doing better. But I'm losing two days a week commuting to this stupid library job in Toronto. I'm already doing a teaching assistantship. I'm not even supposed to have a job outside of school. Because it doesn't go through university payroll, though, they can't do anything about it."

"Why don't you just quit your library job, then?" I said.

Christine's job at the library didn't really help out that much with the bills. She had a twenty-dollar roundtrip commute to Toronto on the GO Bus and she only made about ten dollars an hour. She had to come in two days a week to work for only four hours each day. The only reason that Christine still had the stupid job was because it was a city job and she thought that it might lead to a better job within the municipal government once she graduated with her Master's degree.

Christine didn't like my suggestion that she quit her job. "Quit?" she said. "I just had to pay for another car repair, Jim. I can't quit my job. I know that I don't make much money there, but at this point I feel like anything's helping us."

"I can apply for welfare," I said.

I really didn't want to do this, of course. I hated being on welfare. There was clearly no work for me in Hamilton, though. None of the temp companies that I'd put my name in at had ever called me. Christine was working herself ragged. We needed another source of income. All I had to do was hit up welfare, or Ontario Works, as they called it in Ontario, and we'd get some free money every month. It would help me and Christine out a bit until the spring, when I started working again on the show.

"You're really going to apply for welfare?" Christine said.

"Yeah," I said. "I'll go there today, right after I drop you off."

"OK, I'll give my boss my two weeks' notice tomorrow."

I dropped Christine off at the university and then drove straight to the welfare office. There were several Ontario Works locations in Hamilton. I went to the one on Barton and Nash because it was the one that was closest to our house.

My story for welfare was that I'd been in Alberta for a while and had just come back to Ontario to be closer to my daughter. I had a job lined up, but it didn't start until April. I only needed help from them until then, I told them.

Lying to welfare didn't really bother me. In Ontario they never did home visits. I knew this from the times that I'd collected welfare in my life—the last time being in October 2007—and also from when I was with Nicole, who'd collected the whole time that I was with her. The key was not to tell welfare that I had a girlfriend who I lived with and who had a job. If I'd told them that, I might not have gotten anything, or maybe just a basic needs allowance to cover my own food and clothing. My only option had been to lie. The system practically forced it on me.

Theresa, my caseworker, lapped up my sob story and told me that a cheque would be mailed out to me shortly. I was going to get the maximum rate for a single adult, which was about five hundred and seventy dollars per month. I could have gotten more money if I'd been eligible for a Community Start-Up, which was a benefit that you could get from Ontario Works to cover costs such as moving. I'd already hit welfare up for this in October 2007, though, while living at another Hamilton address. You could only collect it once every two years.

"If you need to keep receiving assistance next month, you'll need to turn in the card that we're going to mail out to you with your cheque," Theresa told me.

I knew all about that card. I thanked Theresa and then left the welfare office.

In three business days, my welfare cheque arrived in the mail. I could have gotten it sooner, by direct deposit, but just like the last time I'd collected welfare, I'd told my worker that I didn't have a bank account. I didn't want to take the chance of them asking to see my bank statements for the previous three months. They would have seen that I'd been in Ontario in November and early December, working temp jobs, not unemployed and living in Alberta at my mom's house, like I'd told them.

As soon as I got my cheque, I went to the TD bank at Centre Mall, paid my car insurance, and then gave two hundred and fifty dollars to Christine to cover my half of the rent for February. Rents in Hamilton were pretty cheap. We only paid five hundred a month for a one-bedroom, plus hydro.

After paying rent and car insurance, I still had some money left, so I called up my weed guy in Hamilton and bought a quarter ounce of weed off him. After that, I was broke. I literally only had a couple dollars left from my cheque.

It didn't really make sense to me, giving Christine money for rent, because as soon as I did, I was basically asking her for it back. The next day, when I drove Christine to school, we stopped at a Petro-Canada and Christine put forty dollars' worth of gas in my tank and agreed to buy me a pack of smokes. This was something that she'd been doing for me for a while—buying me smokes. I found it pretty strange, honestly, that Christine never asked me why I never had money to buy my own smokes. The old guy that I was driving around was supposedly giving me a few bucks for my time. How come I never had any money? I also found it odd that Christine never asked me why she had to fill me up so much, when the guy was also supposedly putting gas in car. I drove Christine around a lot, now that I wasn't working temp jobs anymore, but I didn't drive her around that much. These types of observations made me think of the night that Christine had come into the bathroom while I was in there, smoking crack. I really wasn't sure what was going on inside her head.

While Christine was happy to get some money out of me after I got my welfare cheque, she was still really stressed out about her stats course. She'd given her two weeks' notice at her library job, but she still had to work there until the nineteenth of February. Her midterm was looming and without having enough time to study, she was really worried about it.

At around this time, I started having problems of my own, with Bruce. His drug use was getting pretty bad. When he wasn't smoking crack in my car and at crack houses, he was having me take him back to his place so that he could shoot OxyContin with his junkie wife.

The week that I got my welfare cheque, I went to pick Bruce up one morning to take him to the methadone clinic. He had me come upstairs to his apartment, where I found him crushing up an Oxy on the coffee table.

"Bruce," I said. "What the hell are you doing that shit for right now? I'm about to take you to treatment."

"So?" Bruce said.

I watched Bruce as he finished crushing up the Oxy. When he was done, he cooked it up in a spoon and then drew the liquid up into a syringe. Then he did something really odd, which I could never understand. He got up from where he was sitting and went over to the far corner of the room. There was a big plastic palm tree over there, in between the wall and the couch. Bruce went right up to the tree, squatted down next to it, and then stuck the needle into his vein. It was all pretty disgusting, first thing in the morning.

After Bruce shot up, we went down to the car. Before we even had a chance to get out of the parking lot, Bruce had his crack stem in his hand and was already blasting off.

"You should really cool it with that shit, man," I said. "We're going to be there soon."

"I know," Bruce said. "I just don't want to be on the nod when I get to the clinic."

The day only got worse as it went on. After taking Bruce to the methadone clinic, I drove him around for a couple hours. I wanted to take a break after that, so I dropped Bruce off at a crack house on King Street, and then went home to get high.

About an hour after I got home, Bruce called me, asking me to pick him up.

"OK," I said. "I'll be right over."

"Wait," Bruce said.

"What?"

"I'm not at the house anymore."

"OK. Where are you?"

"I'm down the street, at the motel."

Down the street, at the corner of King and Sanford, was a little L-shaped motel.

Bruce told me the room number that he was in.

"All right," I said, and then hung up the phone.

I drove over to the motel and knocked on Bruce's door.

A few seconds later, Bruce answered the door. He had his phone to his ear and was in the middle of a heated conversation with someone. Behind him, on the bed, were a couple of naked hookers.

Before I could piece together who Bruce was talking to, he hung up the phone abruptly. He looked at me and then motioned to the hookers on the bed. "You want any of that before we take off?" he said.

"Uh, no thanks," I said.

We left the room and went out to my car. We got on the road and Bruce had me drive him to this residential street about five minutes away from the motel.

"OK, pull over," Bruce said.

I pulled the car over to the side of the road. Bruce got out and walked over to a house on the other side of the street.

I immediately assumed that Bruce was having me take him to some crack house. When no one came to the door, though, I knew that something was up.

Bruce kept knocking on the door. "Hey, asshole!" he yelled all of a sudden. "Your car's in the driveway. I know you're fucking home!"

I suddenly realized that the person whose house we were at was probably the same person who Bruce had been talking to on the phone, at the motel.

Bruce banged on the guy's door a few more times and then walked down the driveway, to the car that was parked there. It was an old beater car; a little Honda Civic. Bruce approached the driver's side of the car. He took a step back and then attempted to boot off the driver's side mirror. Bruce wasn't very coordinated, however. He missed the thing and landed flat on his ass. From across the street, this was actually pretty funny.

Bruce quickly got up and made another attempt to boot

the mirror off of the car. This time, his foot connected with the mirror. The thing ripped off the side of the car and went flying off into some bushes.

"Wait until you see what else I'm going to do to your car, motherfucker!" Bruce yelled.

I glanced at the house that Bruce was outside of. I noticed that the curtains in the front room were moving slightly. It was the person who lived there, I realized. He was peeking out through the curtains, watching Bruce destroy his car.

Bruce kept yelling and kicking the crap out of the poor bastard's car. Soon all the dogs in the neighbourhood were going nuts. I could hear a siren off in the distance. Bruce must have heard it, too, because he kicked the car's rear fender one last time, and then quickly came back across the street to where I was parked.

As soon as Bruce got into the car, I freaked out on him. "What the hell is wrong with you?" I said. "Did you fucking lose it or something? It's broad daylight, man. Everyone in this whole fucking neighbourhood saw you do that."

Bruce was surprisingly calm now, as if flipping out like that had enabled him to get whatever was bothering him off of his chest.

"That guy used to be my driver, Jim," Bruce told me. "He drove me around before I met you. He ripped me off for a half-quarter. He told me that he'd pay me back, but he never did. I just wanted to teach him a lesson. It could have been worse. He's lucky he still has his front teeth."

The siren got closer. I didn't have time to respond. I slammed my foot down on the accelerator and burnt rubber as I sped the hell out of there.

I drove Bruce around for a couple more hours and then went home to take another break. Just as I was finished getting high, Christine came home from her job at the library. It was around six o'clock.

I was still stoned when Christine got in the door, so I pretended that I'd been asleep on the couch and was just waking up. Christine came over to me, gave me a kiss, and then went into the kitchen to make supper.

Before supper was ready, Bruce called, asking me to pick him up. I was straight enough to leave the house by this point, but I suddenly had this really bad feeling about driving Bruce somewhere. I had this weird feeling that something bad was going to happen, like he was going to get busted or something. I knew that nothing would happen to me, of course, if Bruce got busted because I wouldn't have any drugs on me, or in my car. I just didn't want the hassle if I could avoid it.

I decided to listen to my gut and told Bruce that I couldn't drive him. I didn't tell him that I'd never drive him again; I just told him that I couldn't drive him that night.

Bruce got really pissed off. "What do you mean, you can't drive me tonight?" he said.

"I've got things to do," I said.

"What things? Quit fucking around, Jim. I need you to pick me up."

"Look, buddy, I think you're going to be taking the bus."

I hung up the phone as Bruce screeched at me. I put the phone on mute and then put it down on the coffee table. The phone started vibrating a few second later. I reached for it and turned it off.

Soon, supper was ready. I sat down with Christine at the table and picked at my food because I'd just gotten high and wasn't hungry.

After supper, Christine did some studying. I sat down on

the love seat and cleaned out my stem with rubbing alcohol. Because Christine thought that I used the stem only to smoke weed with, she naturally assumed that what I was scraping off the plate was resin. It obviously didn't occur to her that resin was gooey; it didn't flake off ceramic the way crack did. The only thing that I had to hide from Christine was when I melted the scrapings into my screen. When I did this, it made the end of my stem look really shiny. I was always afraid that Christine would notice this and realize that it wasn't marijuana resin that I was about to smoke, that it was something else. To be on the safe side, I went into the kitchen for a second to melt the scrapings into my screen. Then I came back into the living room.

I got a good hoot, but it wore off quickly. It wasn't long before I wanted to get high again. No longer caring about the bad feeling I'd had earlier, I picked up the phone and called Bruce. Bruce wouldn't answer his phone, though.

Great, I thought. Now he's ignoring you.

I was so desperate to get high that I decided to just ask Christine if she'd lend me sixty bucks. I only needed fifty— enough for a forty piece, plus a tip for Chester or Sal—but I knew that we'd have to go to the bank machine, which only dispensed twenty-dollar bills, since Christine didn't keep that much money in her purse.

"What do you need sixty bucks for?" Christine asked me.

"I want to get some weed," I said.

"What about the guy that you've been driving? I thought that he was paying you a few bucks or whatever to drive him around."

Hearing Christine say this kind of surprised me. It was the first time that she was asking me why I didn't have any money, when the guy that I was driving was supposedly paying me for my time.

I quickly made up a lie to account for why I didn't have any money. "He was short on cash this past week, so we started a tab," I said.

"How big is the tab?" Christine said.

"I don't know . . . about a hundred and fifty dollars."

Christine's jaw dropped. "Are you kidding me?" she said. "Jim, how could you let this guy jack up a tab like that?"

"We did it before and he paid me back," I said. "I don't know what happened this time. He won't answer his phone all of a sudden. It's really unlike him. I think that maybe he got busted or something."

"Well, that's just great. This guy owes you money and now he's probably in jail. You're always telling me that you're so street smart. Well, you know what? That wasn't very street smart, Jim. That was actually pretty stupid!"

Christine tossed the book that she was reading onto the coffee table. Then she went into the kitchen and started doing the dishes.

I picked up the phone and tried calling up Bruce again. He still wouldn't answer his phone.

Seeing as how Christine obviously wasn't going to give me any money, I decided to just go over to Chester's house to see if anyone had seen Bruce around. If I couldn't find Bruce, I was just going to ask Chester if he could hook me up with another dealer who needed a driver.

As I put on my coat, in the kitchen, I apologized to Christine. "Baby, I'm sorry," I said. "I shouldn't have asked you for money. I'm going to go over to buddy's house right now. I'll talk to his wife. I'm sure that she'll know where he is."

Christine was so pissed off at me that she barely even

acknowledged the apology. "Yeah, whatever," she said, as she scrubbed a dinner plate. "I'll see you when you get home."

I left the house and drove over to Chester's. As soon as I got there, I immediately found out why I couldn't get a hold of Bruce.

"Didn't you hear?" Sal said. "Bruce just got busted."

"Busted?" I said. "What do you mean? I just talked to him a couple of hours ago."

"Yeah, it just happened. He was apparently coming back from his dealer's house when the cops jacked him up. I was wondering what the hell happened to you. I thought you might have been driving him."

"I decided not to tonight."

"Well, aren't you lucky?"

Chester turned the volume down on his TV, and then turned to me. "Hey, Jim," he said.

"Yeah, what?" I said.

"That newspaper box is *still* in my basement!"

I was jonesing so bad that I nearly bit the old man's head off. "Yeah, and what the hell do you want me to do about it right now?" I said. "I hate to tell you, but I think you're beat, bud."

Sal asked me if I needed another dealer to drive around.

"Yeah," I said. "Do you know anybody?"

"I know this kid who lives in Burlington," Sal said. "He might be able to use a driver."

"Is he another whackjob?"

"No."

"Good. Call him up."

Sal called up the dealer. A few minutes later, we went out to meet him.

The dealer turned out to be this white kid in his early

twenties, who called himself Pablo. Pablo gave Sal a tip for hooking him up with me. I drove back to Chester's house, dropped off Sal, and then got back on the road.

I immediately laid down the law with Pablo. "This is how this is going to work, OK?" I told him. "I get ten dollars an hour, but you've got to pay me in crack. Don't pay me until the end of the night, when I drop you off, and keep your dope on your person at all times. You got that?"

"Yeah," Pablo said.

"Oh, and one more thing: don't ever smoke crack in my car."

"You don't have to worry about that. I don't smoke this shit, I just sell it."

"Well, that's good to hear."

I drove Pablo around for a few hours. Absolutely no funny stuff happened. It was actually pretty boring, compared to driving Bruce. This, however, was a good thing. I didn't want any drama; I just wanted my piece at the end of the night. Even though Pablo sold his dope the same way that Bruce did—by breaking off little pieces by eyeing them—he never did any drugs in my car, nor did any of his customers. One of his customers even bought ten dollars' worth of crack and paid for it in change and Pablo let me keep the change for gas money.

At around midnight, I dropped Pablo off at an apartment building in Burlington. He lived right off the QEW, on North Shore Boulevard.

Pablo gave me my piece. It was a really good count.

"I'll call you tomorrow, OK?" Pablo said.

I knew that in the morning, I'd wake up, telling myself that I wasn't going to get high that day. Like every other morning, though, I knew that I'd end up doing it.

"All right," I said.

I jumped back on the QEW. In less than fifteen minutes, I was home.

As soon as I got in the door, Christine asked me about the old guy I'd been driving. "Did you find out what happened to him?" she said.

I made up a bullshit story. "Yeah, I went over to his house and talked to his wife," I said. "She told me that he got arrested today and that he's in jail right now. It wasn't for drugs or anything like that, though; it was for public drunkenness. The guy's a huge drunk. I'm constantly taking him to the liquor store. His wife said that he should be out of jail in the morning. This kind of thing happens to him all the time, apparently."

"Well, I'm glad to hear that he'll be getting out of jail tomorrow," Christine said. "Maybe tomorrow, when he gets out, you can get him to pay back the money that he owes you. You shouldn't let him run up a tab like that again, Jim."

"Yeah, I know," I said.

To make Christine feel better, the next day, I told her that I'd managed to get in touch with the old guy. I told her that he'd paid back the money he owed me and that I wasn't going to drive him anymore.

"Good," Christine said. "Does that mean you're going to look for a regular job now?"

"No," I said.

Christine's face sunk with disappointment.

"I'm going to be driving my weed guy around," I said.

"Your weed guy?" Christine said. "I hope you're not planning on taking this guy to his dealer's house to pick up weed or whatever."

"Relax," I said. "I won't be doing anything like that, Christine. I'm just going to be driving him around so that he can get places, like to his girlfriend's house in Brantford, and to help him run errands and stuff. He already knows not to bring any drugs into my car. I told him that as soon as I agreed to drive him."

"OK," Christine said, even though she still didn't seem too happy with the arrangement. "As long as this guy knows that he's never to bring any drugs into your car, I guess it's all right."

10

A few days after I started driving Pablo, Christine had her Reading Week. It was now the middle of February. I was hoping that Christine would relax during her week off from school and spend some time studying for her stats midterm, which she was still really worried about it. The week, however, turned out to be anything but relaxing. It started off with Christine getting an angry phone call from her parents about her cell phone bill. The bill, apparently, had come to about three hundred dollars.

Christine was on the phone with her parents for about half an hour. When she finally got off the phone, she immediately turned to me and told me about the bill.

"I told you to watch how many minutes you were using," Christine said. "You went way over the limit!"

I wasn't surprised that I'd gone over Christine's talk-time limit. She didn't get too many daytime minutes and what few she had, she had to share with her sister. What surprised me was how much I'd gone over. I honestly didn't think I'd used up that many minutes.

"I don't know what happened," I said. "I always made sure to keep the calls really short."

"Yeah, well those short calls added up," Christine said. "My parents said that the record of calls was over a page long."

"Tell your parents that I'll pay them back this summer, when I'm working."

"I'm not even going to bother, Jim. They won't take your money. They won't even take mine. I already offered to pay the bill, but my mom told me that she knows that I don't have that kind of money right now because I'm in school. She said that my dad is going to pay the bill this week at the bank."

Christine's phone was sitting in the middle of the coffee table. She reached her arm out suddenly and snatched it off the table. "You're not allowed to use this thing anymore, OK?" she said. "I can't risk getting another phone bill like that."

"So I can't even make a phone call now?" I said.

"Not on my phone, you can't. In fact, I don't think that I can even use this thing anymore. We're already into the next billing cycle. You've probably already used up all my minutes."

Christine was so paranoid about us using the cell phone that she immediately called a phone company and asked to have a landline installed.

"This way, we can make as many local calls as we want, and we don't have to worry about how many minutes we're using," Christine told me after she got off the phone with the phone company.

We didn't have a phone jack in our apartment, so the phone company had to send a technician over. The technician wasn't due to show up until Wednesday, which was two days later. I had no way of getting in touch with Pablo during this time, other than to tell him that I wouldn't be reachable for a couple of days, so the minute I started jonesing, I took my laptop downtown to a pawn shop, put it on loan for a hundred dollars, and then went to Chester's and bought a forty piece. I didn't feel too bad about putting my computer on loan because I wasn't using it much anyway. I'd been spending all of my time driving Pablo around and getting high. It didn't make a difference to me if my computer was sitting in a pawn shop. At home, it was just collecting dust. I figured that Christine probably wouldn't even notice that it was gone. As long as I paid the ten dollars in interest every month, I wouldn't lose my computer.

On Wednesday morning the technician from the phone company came over and installed the landline. As soon as the installation was done and the guy left the apartment, I took the cheap, cordless phone that Christine had bought at Walmart with me the day before and called Pablo on it.

Pablo didn't recognize the new phone number. "Who's this?" he said.

"It's Jim," I said. "I've got a new number."

"Cool. I'll add it to my contacts. Can you pick me up right now? I've got some stuff to do."

"Yeah, sure."

I hung up the phone and went into the kitchen. I started to put on my coat.

"You're going out?" Christine said.

"Yeah, my weed guy wants me to drive him to Brantford to visit his girlfriend," I said.

"OK. While you're gone, maybe I'll wash the floor."

I left the apartment and drove over to Pablo's building. When Pablo got into the car, I explained to him about the new phone number.

"It's actually a landline," I said. "I don't have a cell phone right now. You have to call the home number. If you call, and my girlfriend answers, just ask for me, OK?"

"Your girlfriend won't ask me who I am, or why I'm calling?" Pablo said.

"No. She doesn't screen my calls, man. It ain't like you're a broad calling. She already knows that I'm driving some guy around. She thinks that you're my weed guy and that I'm driving you around all the time to help you run errands and stuff."

Pablo got a pretty good kick out of this. "Really?" he said, laughing. "She believes that?"

"Yeah," I said. "She has no idea about my drug habit. I'm trying to keep it on the down low, if you know what I mean."

"OK, that's cool. Are you sure that you're going to be reachable on a landline, though? What if I call you and you're not home?"

"I'm always home. Unless I'm driving you somewhere, I'll be at home. The only exception to that is on Mondays, Tuesdays, and Wednesdays, when I pick up my girlfriend from university at around five o'clock."

"OK. That sounds good."

On Thursday that week, Christine went to Toronto to work her last shift at the library. While Christine was at work, I drove Pablo around.

After the deliveries were done, I told Pablo that we could go back to my place on a break, instead of me dropping him off at some crack house somewhere like I usually did.

It meant a lot less driving for me, and thus a lot less gas being used, since I didn't have to pick Pablo up where I'd dropped him off and then take him to his next drug deal. We could just go straight there from my place.

"What about your girlfriend?" Pablo said.

"She's out of town for the day," I said.

Even though I barely knew Pablo, I trusted him enough to let him come over to my house for a couple of hours. With Christine in Toronto, there was absolutely no risk. I was even able to do a couple of hoots with Pablo sitting there and didn't feel any more paranoid than I usually did when I smoked crack. Pablo didn't smoke crack, of course, so he just hung out and watched TV.

Once the high wore off and some customers had called, we left the house to make some more deliveries. A couple of hours later, we went back to my place and I did a couple more hoots. Then we went back out again . . .

11

On the twenty-fifth of February I got my next welfare cheque in the mail. I gave two hundred and fifty dollars to Christine to cover my half of March rent, and then went to the bank and paid my car insurance.

A few days later, on the second of March, the landlords came by to collect the rent. It was the evening and I had just gotten home with Christine from the university.

I took the rent cheque off of the light switch in the kitchen and gave it to Harriet.

"We've got some good news for you," Harriet said.

"Oh, yeah?" I said. "What?"

"We managed to get some more funding for renovations. We're going to be fixing your kitchen floor."

I was pretty surprised to hear this. I was expecting to have to nag the landlords about my floor for at least another couple of months.

"That's great," I said. "When are you guys going to do it?"

"We're going to do it this week," Harriet said. "Rajeev's going to pick up the tiles tomorrow. We were thinking of coming by on Wednesday."

"OK. What time?"

"How's noon?"

Having the landlords come by at this time would kill my afternoon because it meant that I wouldn't be able to go out and drive Pablo. I never liked anyone being in my apartment when I wasn't home, even my landlords. It was a small price to pay, though, for a new floor.

"That's fine," I said. "Noon's good."

On Wednesday, before the landlords came over, I drove Christine to the university. She had to hand in her stats midterm, which had been a take-home exam. Even though Christine had worked on the exam for an entire week, she struggled up until the last minute to finish it. Ten minutes before we left the house, she was printing it off the computer.

After I'd dropped Christine off, I went home to wait for the landlords to show up. At a quarter to twelve, they came to the door.

Rajeev and Harriet immediately began working on the floor. They pulled up all of the linoleum and then put down grey ceramic tiles.

When the floor was finally done, there was a space measuring a couple of square feet that didn't have any tiles on it.

"Sorry, Jim, but we ran out of tiles," Rajeev told me. "I thought that we had some more in the truck, but they're actually a different colour. I'll have to order some more of these grey ones."

The spot that was missing tiles just so happened to be right where the stove went. The next night, after I'd cleaned the grout off the floor and I'd put the fridge and the stove back, part of the stove was on tiles and the other half wasn't so it kept teetering.

"They should have just left the floor the way it was," Christine said. "I don't even like these tiles, honey. You can't stand on them without slippers. They're freezing."

I was pissed off about the wobbly stove, too, but the tiles were so much better than the linoleum. There was no denying it.

"You'll feel better about the floor once the landlords finish the job," I said. "You just need to get used to it."

Christine glanced at the floor and then made a face. "I guess so," she said.

The landlords didn't get back to me about finishing our floor right away. I thought about calling them, but I didn't want to get on their case. I was just happy that they'd done anything at all, even if the job they'd done had been sort of half-assed. I knew that they would finish the floor eventually. It would just take them a while to get around to it. It's how they were with everything.

A week after getting the new floor, Christine got her stats midterm back. She ended up doing all right.

"See, what'd I tell you?" I said, as I picked her up that day and we were on our way home from the university. "You did fine. You worried yourself sick for nothing."

"I still only got an A-minus," Christine said.

"So? What's wrong with that? That's a good grade. I wish I would have gotten some A-minuses in school."

"Honey, in grad school, getting an A-minus is like getting a C."

"Well, you've got some room for improvement, then. You

have more time to study now that you don't have that library job. I bet that by the time you go to write your final exam, you'll get an A-plus."

Christine laughed at me and rolled her eyes. "OK, let's not go nuts," she said.

We drove home and Christine made supper. I waited around for Pablo to call. While I waited, I went on Christine's laptop and checked my email and my Facebook page. I usually checked them every couple of days.

There was a new message for me on Facebook:

Hey what's up with your phone? Do you not want to be in contact with your kid anymore or something?

The message was from Nicole. I hadn't talked to her since that day in January, when I'd told her that I couldn't see my daughter yet because I wasn't working. She'd obviously tried to call my cell phone number and realized that the number had been disconnected.

I immediately posted a reply to Nicole's message on Facebook:

Nicole, I still want to see my kid. I just don't have a working phone right now ok? Tell Emily that I love her and that I'll see her as soon as I can. If you need to reach me and it's urgent please call my mom.

I didn't want to give Nicole our home number because I was sure that if I did, Christine would have freaked out.

Before supper was ready, Pablo called, asking me to pick him up.

"OK, I'll be right over," I said, and then hung up the phone.

I went into the kitchen. Christine had just taken some chicken legs out of the oven and was flipping them over with a pair of tongs.

"Who was that on the phone?" Christine said.

"Oh, just my weed guy," I said.

I started to put on my coat.

"You're going out?"

"Yeah, he wants me to drive him somewhere."

Christine turned and went back to flipping the chicken. "OK, love you," she said. "See you when you get home."

12

The day after getting Nicole's message on Facebook, Dave dropped by unexpectedly. It was the afternoon and I was on a break from driving Pablo. I'd just finished smoking a twenty piece in the bathroom and I was lying down on the loveseat. Christine was sitting on the couch, studying.

Dave brought a joint with him. He lit it up and immediately got into the reason why he'd come over.

"I just got jobs for both of us," Dave said.

"Jobs?" I said. "What kind of jobs?"

"Working at the Woodbine in Toronto."

The Woodbine was a racetrack in northwest Toronto. I couldn't imagine what the hell kind of work Dave had gotten for us up there.

"There's a big mall up there," Dave said. "It's called the Woodbine Centre. It's got a year-round indoor carnival. I was just talking to Bob Shelley today. He said he's got a couple of joints up there."

To me, it sounded like a blank—as in that there was very little money to be made there. I figured that a carnival that was in a mall year-round would get pretty tiresome to the people who shopped their regularly after a while. Dave tried to convince me that it was worth it.

"I'm not going to lie to you," Dave said. "It is a blank during the week, when people are at work and the kids are at school. But on the weekends it's pretty good, apparently. This would only be for the weekends."

"How many points is Bobby going to pay us?"

"Twenty."

Twenty percent commission was about what the average small show paid.

"OK," I said. "I'll do it."

On Saturday, instead of driving Pablo around, I got up in the morning and drove to Toronto to work at the Woodbine with Dave. The Woodbine turned out to be a pretty good spot. There were a lot of people with kids that day at the mall. Dave and I were in a mini basketball joint, which was great because it's a build-up game, or "prize every time" game. These were the types of games that I usually worked in. You could get a lot of money out of people if you ran a collection.

While the money was good, what pissed me off about working at the Woodbine was Dave. As soon as I got in the joint with him, he started getting all competitive with me. It reminded me of how much I hated working alongside him during the summer on the show, especially when I was out-grossing him. Dave was really competitive in the joint. He couldn't stand it if anyone was out-grossing him.

At one point, I called in some customers and Dave tried

to lure one of them over to his counter. After I'd finished dealing with the customers, and they'd walked away from my counter, I turned to Dave. "Hey, what the fuck, man?" I said. "Get your own fucking mooches, bud."

Dave acted like he didn't know what I was talking about. He grinned at me and then called someone in.

At three o'clock, when I finally got my break, I couldn't wait to get out of the joint and get away from Dave. I went straight to the mall food court and got something to eat. I paid for the food with money that I'd skimmed from the apron. I always took my skim off the low-end stock, meaning that if I got fifteen dollars for a piece of stock and I only needed ten dollars to cover my stock average, I'd put the fin in my pocket.

After I finished eating, I went outside and had a smoke. Then I got back in the joint. I got each of the next three customers I called in for a big one—a piece of stock worth at least fifty bucks.

That night Dave and I finished work at seven o'clock. After we counted the stock and locked up the joint, Bob paid us under the table, in cash. Including what I stole, I managed to walk out of there with about two hundred bucks.

We left the Woodbine and drove back to Hamilton. On the way home, we stopped at a Petro-Canada to fill up. Dave chipped in for gas. Now that we were out of the joint and we weren't competing with each other, Dave was treating me like a friend again and not like a rival salesman.

When we got back to Hamilton, I went home to call up Pablo. I'd been thinking about getting high ever since I'd left the Woodbine and I wanted to buy a forty piece off him.

"How was work?" Christine said when I got in the door.

"Shitty," I said.

"Why? What happened?"

"Oh, nothing. It just wasn't very good there. I didn't make much money."

I didn't want to tell Christine about the money I'd made because I knew that if I did, she would have expected me to give her some of it to help out with the bills. It was shitty of me, but I didn't want to have to do that. I'd been broke for so long that it was nice to finally have some money for myself.

Christine went back to her studying. I took the cordless phone into the bathroom and called up Pablo.

"Hey, can I get a four off you?" I said.

"Yeah, sure," Pablo said. "Then can you drive me somewhere? I've got to get across town."

"All right, but then I've got to go home, OK? I just worked all day, man. I'm pretty tired."

Pablo told me where to meet him. It was some crack house downtown.

"OK, I'll see you in a few minutes," I said.

I hung up the phone, took a piss, and then came out of the bathroom.

"Baby, I've got to go out right now," I said. "My weed guy wants me to drive him across town."

"OK," Christine said.

In the morning Dave and I went back to work at the Woodbine. The mall was really busy again. The Sunday shift wasn't as long as the Saturday shift, so I didn't make as much money as I'd made on Saturday, but I still managed to walk out of there with about a hundred and fifty bucks.

While I was at work that day, I went to a cell phone kiosk

in the mall during my break and bought myself a phone. Even though it was working out all right having Pablo call me on the home phone, I still wanted to have a cell phone.

The phone was just your basic flip phone. It was normally a hundred-dollar phone, but it was on sale for fifty bucks. It was a new cell phone company and they were offering per-second billing and no system access fees, which was a pretty good deal.

That night, when Dave and I got back to Hamilton, I dropped Dave off and then called up Pablo.

"Hey, it's Jim," I said. "I've got a new number again."

"Cool," Pablo said. "I'll update you in my contacts."

"It's a cell phone, by the way. Don't call the home number anymore, all right? Just call the cell from now on."

"All right. What do you want, a four?"

"Yeah. Where are you?"

"Same place as last night."

"OK. I'll be there in a few minutes."

I drove downtown and got my dope off Pablo. I went home and immediately went into the bathroom to get high.

Later that night, before going to bed, I showed Christine the cell phone I'd bought. I made sure to tell her how cheap I'd gotten it for, though. I also told her that after buying the phone, and after activating it, I didn't have much left from my pay.

Christine didn't seem too interested in the phone. She didn't even ask to look at it. "That's nice, honey," she said. "I'm glad you've got a phone again."

"Yeah, it'll be easier to keep in touch with my weed guy now," I said.

On Monday morning I got up and drove Christine to school. After that, at around eleven o'clock, I drove to Burlington and picked up Pablo. We made some deliveries and when we were done, I decided to go back to my place with Pablo on a break. I felt a little paranoid doing this, since Christine was only a short distance away, at the university. We were right by the house, though, and I wanted to get high.

As Pablo was giving me my piece to smoke, I cracked to him about the way he sold his dope. "You know, you're really ripping yourself off by dealing your shit that way," I told him.

"What do you mean?" Pablo said.

"You just break off pieces by eyeing them. You could be off by five or ten bucks."

Pablo had just broken off a twenty piece for me. "Does this not look like twenty bucks' worth to you?" he said.

"It does," I said. "I'm just saying, man. I think it would be easier if you used a scale."

I went into the bedroom and got my digital scale. I had the thing for selling weed to the guys on the show in the summertime. The scale measured to three decimal places, which wasn't necessary if you were just selling weed. I'd bought it, though, because it just so happened to be cheaper than the one that measured to two decimal places for some reason.

I brought the scale back to the living room and handed it to Pablo.

Pablo looked at the scale. "Why do you have a scale like this?" he said.

I didn't want to tell Pablo what I did for a living, and therefore why I had the scale—I didn't want to get too personal with him—so I just made something up.

"Someone owed me some money one time," I said. "They couldn't afford to pay me back, so they gave me this thing. You can use it if you want."

"Thanks," Pablo said. "How much do you want for it?"

"Nothing. I'm not giving it to you, man; I'm just lending it. Think of it as me doing you a favour. I'm just trying to help you out so that you don't rip yourself off."

"Oh, OK," Pablo said.

Pablo put the scale down on the coffee table. He picked up the TV remote and then turned on the TV.

While Pablo watched TV, I went into the bathroom, got my stem, and then sat down on the couch and smoked the dope that Pablo had given me.

By the time that I was done smoking, and I was straight enough to leave the house, some customers had called. Pablo put the digital scale in his pocket and we went out to make the deliveries.

That night, after dropping Pablo off in Burlington, I went home and got high, as usual. When I was done, I decided to call up Pablo and buy more dope off him. I'd already smoked almost a hundred dollars' worth of crack that day, but after doing a few blasts in a row, I wanted to get more dope, and because I had money from the Woodbine, I was able to get more.

Because I'd just smoked, I was feeling really paranoid. I had some weed in the house, so I had a couple of tokes to help get rid of the paranoia.

When I felt OK to leave the house, I called up Pablo.

Pablo was kind of pissed off that I was calling him up so late. "Jim, what do you want?" he said. "It's two o'clock in the morning."

"Can I get a four off you?" I said.

"Seriously? I just got into bed."

"Sorry, man. I really fucking need it."

"OK, fine. When are you going to get over here?"

"I'm leaving the house right now."

"All right. I'll come down and meet you in the lobby."

Christine had already gone to bed. After checking on her to make sure that she was still asleep, I put on my coat, closed the door as quietly as possible, and then went down to my car.

When I got over to Pablo's building, Pablo was waiting for me in the lobby. His building had one of those roundabout driveways out front, so all I had to do was jump out of my car, get my dope, and drive off. It was easier than going through the drive-thru at a McDonald's.

After buying dope off Pablo that night, I started doing it every night. Even though I'd made a few hundred dollars at the Woodbine, by the end of the week, I was broke.

On Friday night I wanted to buy more dope, after smoking the piece that Pablo had given me for driving him around. Because I didn't have any money, though, I just shoved the thought aside and got into bed with Christine.

Before we went to sleep, Christine wanted to have sex. I was still high from the crack I'd just smoked, however, and wasn't in the mood. Unlike some people, I never got a sex buzz when I smoked crack. All I was in the mood for was to call up Pablo and buy more dope.

I didn't want Christine to think that something was wrong, so I gave her some cock just to make her happy. It took a lot longer than normal for my dick to get hard because of the crack I'd just smoked. Christine didn't seem to notice, though. Once I was hard, we fucked like we normally did.

After we had sex and we were lying in bed, I was still thinking about getting high. I decided to just roll over and ask Christine if she'd lend me some money. I wanted to get some "weed," I told her.

I was expecting Christine to ask me why I didn't have

money to buy weed myself. I'd been driving around my "weed guy" all week, after all, who was supposedly paying me for my time. Christine didn't ask about this, though. She was only concerned with the fact that it was late and that we'd have to go to the bank machine.

"You seriously want to go to the bank machine right now?" Christine said.

"Yeah," I said.

"Honey, it's two o'clock in the morning."

"You don't have to come with me if you don't want to."

"How do you figure that?"

"Just give me your bank card and tell me your PIN."

Christine wasn't comfortable with this idea. "That's OK," she said. "I'll come with you to the bank."

At first, Christine didn't seem to mind going with me to the bank machine. It wasn't until we were actually in the car, on our way over there, that she started to seem pissed off. I think that it must have finally sunk in that what we were doing wasn't normal; it was kind of fucked up.

"I can't believe that we're going to the bank right now," Christine said, as we sat at a light. "It's the middle of the night. You shouldn't be doing this kind of crap to me, Jim. If you wanted money, you should have asked me for it when you got home from driving that guy around. You shouldn't have waited until we went to bed."

I didn't say a thing. I just let Christine bitch. I knew that anything I said would have resulted in an argument and I didn't want that. Christine hadn't given me the money yet.

When we got to the bank, Christine took sixty dollars out of the machine. I only needed forty, but the last time I'd asked Christine for money for weed, I'd asked for sixty. Even though she hadn't ended up giving it to me, I wanted to be consistent.

Christine gave me the money and then I dropped her off at home.

As soon as Christine was out of the car, I called up Pablo.

"Jim, do you realize what time it is?" Pablo said.

"I know," I said. "I'm sorry, man. I just want another four."

"Yeah, fine. I'll meet you in the lobby."

"Great. I'll be right over."

I gave Pablo forty dollars and he gave me my piece. Normally, Pablo gave me really good counts, but this one was kind of small.

"Hey, what's with this shitty count, man?" I said.

"Sorry, Jim," Pablo said. "I don't have that much dope left on me right now. I didn't expect to start smoking my own stuff. I still have a few more deliveries to make tonight."

I knew that Pablo wasn't bullshitting me. He usually only carried around as much dope as he was planning on selling, plus whatever he had to give me.

"OK, whatever," I said. "Don't worry about it. Just make it up to me later."

"Don't worry," Pablo said. "I will."

In the morning I went back to work at the Woodbine with Dave. As usual, I made good money there.

When I got back to Hamilton that night, I called up Pablo. I couldn't get a hold of him, though, for some reason, so I had to go to Chester's.

On my way over to Chester's, I stopped at a convenience store to get a pack of smokes and a lighter. As I was leaving the store, I tore the cellophane off of the pack of smokes, and then walked over to a trashcan a few feet from the entrance to chuck it.

Some guy approached me while I was at the trashcan. I recognized him as one of Pablo's regular customers.

"Hey, have you seen Pablo?" the guy asked me.

"Sorry," I said. "I haven't seen him today."

Suddenly, without warning, the guy reached out and grabbed me by the collar of my jacket. The pack of smokes in my hand went flying as the guy shoved me up against the front of the convenience store.

"Don't fuck around with me, buddy!" the guy yelled. "I

know that you're Pablo's driver. Where the fuck is he?"

The guy had me pinned against the glass by my shoulders. He reached into his pocket, pulled out a small knife, and held it to my throat. "*Now* are you ready to tell me where Pablo is?" he said.

I was stunned. I seriously thought the guy was going to cut me. He was holding the blade to my throat with so much pressure that I literally thought that it would pop right through the skin. Inside the convenience store, I could hear the clerk yelling. In broken English, he was screaming about how he was going to call the cops. The guy with the knife ignored him.

It was hard to speak, or even breathe, with the knife against my throat, but I managed to choke out a few words. "I don't know where Pablo is," I said. "Just put the knife away . . . we can talk about this."

The guy stared at me hard for a few seconds. His eyes were red and bulging. "If you know where he is, you better fucking tell me right now," he said. "I'm dead serious."

"I already told you," I said. "I don't know where he is. It's the fucking truth, man! I swear to you on my kid."

Suddenly, the guy's grip on me loosened. "OK," he said. "I believe you."

The guy let me go and put the knife back in his pocket. I tried to calm down, but I was still pretty freaked out.

"The next time you see Pablo, tell him Ronnie's looking for him," the guy said.

"All right," I said. "I will. Do you mind telling me what all this is about?"

"Yeah, your boy Pablo ripped me off last night for a fifty piece. I didn't find out until I got home that it was a piece of fucking soap."

I couldn't believe what I was hearing. "Soap?" I said.

"Yeah, soap!" the guy said. "Like the kind that you have in your bathroom. I should have known when I saw Pablo getting high on his own shit last night to check the piece that he gave me. I was in such a hurry to get home, though, once I had the piece in my hand—you know how it is—that I didn't bother to check."

"I can't believe Pablo did that to you."

"Yeah, well, you obviously don't know Pablo too well. He's a fucking goof, man. He's done this to people before, it's just never happened to me."

Goof. It was one of the worst insults that you could call a person. In the Canadian prison system, if you called someone a goof, it was the same thing as calling someone a bitch in a U.S. prison.

The guy took off across the parking lot. For about a minute, I just stood there in front of the convenience store, waiting for the shock that I was feeling to wear off.

When I finally felt better, I picked up my smokes from off the ground, got into my car, and drove over to Chester's.

As soon as I got to Chester's, I told Sal what happened.

"Yeah, Pablo does that every once in a while," Sal said. "But don't worry. He always comes around later and pays everyone back. Do you need someone else to drive around in the meantime?"

"No," I said. "I've got money tonight."

Sal finished his beer and then we went out to meet the dealer. The dealer sold me a forty piece. I gave Sal a tip, dropped him off, and then went home.

About an hour after I was done smoking the forty piece, I went back to Chester's and bought another forty piece. By the time I was done smoking that, it was time for bed.

Christine fell asleep quickly, but I had some trouble. My

heart was beating way too fast. I was still coming down off the crack high. I kept staring up at the ceiling and thinking about the guy who'd pulled the knife on me earlier, and about how angry I was at Pablo for putting me in that situation.

Suddenly, a creepy thought entered my mind:

What if one of those customers that Pablo ripped off knows where you live?

The thought really worried me even though I knew that it was irrational. None of those people knew where I lived. The guy at the convenience store just lived in the neighbourhood and had just so happened to be walking by the store when he recognized my car. He hadn't been out on a mission to jump me and put a knife to my throat. He'd just happened to run into me and went a little berserk.

Still, I kept worrying. An hour passed. I was still thinking these unsettling thoughts, when I suddenly heard a strange noise in the apartment. It sounded like a deadbolt lock sliding back into a door frame.

I sat bolt upright in bed and literally stopped breathing. I listened for what seemed like twenty minutes, but I didn't hear the noise again. The house was completely silent.

I took a deep breath and relaxed into the pillow.

There's no one in here, I told myself. Everything's fine. You're letting your imagination run away with you.

After a while, I almost managed to drift off. Then I heard another noise. This noise sounded like someone was outside our apartment and had just opened our door. My pulse jacked up. I sat up in bed again.

Someone's in here, I thought. Someone just broke in.

I should have talked myself down from this crazy bullshit, but I was so caught up in my paranoid train of thought that I totally went with it.

Just then, I heard another noise. It sounded like a pair of feet creeping slowly across the living room floor. I nearly jumped right out of bed.

I turned to Christine and shook her. I tried to whisper, but the sound that came out of me was more like a croak.

Christine rolled over and opened her eyes. "Jim?" she said. "Honey, what's wrong?"

"I think there's someone in the house," I said.

Christine must have felt the tremors that were running through my body because her eyes opened wide and she sat right up in bed.

I scanned around the dark room and realized that I needed a weapon. If this guy had a gun, I knew that we were done for. If he had bat or a knife, we at least had a fighting chance.

My eyes settled on the lamp next to the bed. I threw off the covers, got out of bed, and grabbed it. The lamp had a heavy, metal base—perfect for bashing someone over the head with. I unplugged the lamp and quietly removed the shade.

Christine started to get out of bed.

"What are you doing?" I hissed. "Get back into bed!"

Christine shrunk back onto the bed. Her eyes were wide and terrified.

"Just stay here and be quiet, OK?" I said. "I'm going to go out there and handle this. Don't leave this room until I tell you that it's safe."

I wrapped the electrical cord around my fist and hoisted the base of lamp into the air. I crept towards the door. As I reached for the doorknob, an extremely loud noise erupted from behind the door. This time, Christine and I both heard it.

"Oh, my god!" Christine said. "Jim, did you hear that?"

I looked over my shoulder at Christine. She was sitting on the bed with her knees clutched to her chest.

I reached for the doorknob again and turned it. I pulled the door open very slowly and looked out into the living room. I couldn't see a thing, though. It was fucking pitch black.

I took a shaky step over the threshold and remembered having this horrible feeling that there was someone lurking right outside the door, waiting to bash my head in, or blow my brains out. I braced for it, as I took another step, but nothing happened.

"I've got a gun," I said.

The sound of my own voice seemed to echo in the room. It didn't even sound like my own voice speaking. The feeling was surreal.

"You better get out of here, man, because I've got a gun."

My eyes started to adjust to the darkness and I was becoming able to see the vague outlines of the furniture in our living room. To my left was the tall back of the loveseat with its rounded arms, and to my right, the shiny surface of the TV screen. I walked slowly through the room, ready to take a skull-cracking swing with every step.

When I got to the kitchen, I reached for the light switch. While gripping the lamp firmly in my hand, and bracing for violence, I heard the *flick* sound of the light switch, and then the light came on. I looked around, startled by the emptiness of my own kitchen.

I crept towards the apartment door, listening for a moment to see if I could hear anyone on the other side of it, in the stairwell. I reached for the knob and yanked the door open. The light above the landing flickered as cold air rushed in, at my face. When I looked around, though, peering down the stairs to the street door, there was no one in the stairwell. I breathed a huge sigh of relief and felt the lamp slip from my hand and fall to the floor.

A creaking noise came from inside the apartment suddenly. I spun around, fumbling for the lamp, but saw that it was only Christine, peering out from behind the bedroom door like a scared child who'd just had a bad dream. Christine said something to me, but it was so low that I could barely hear it.

I let the lamp drop to the floor again. "It's OK, baby," I said. "There's no one in here. You can come out now."

"But I heard a noise, Jim," Christine said. "We both heard it."

"I know, but there's no one in here. I checked."

Christine came slowly out of the bedroom, as if she still didn't trust that it was safe. She sat down on the couch and stared at me. The colour was completely drained from her face.

I sat down beside Christine and for a while, we both sat there, not saying anything. Then we heard the noise again.

The closet! I thought.

There was a closet right when you came into our apartment, by the door. It was small, but there was enough space in there for someone to hide under the coats.

I darted back into the kitchen and flung open the closet door. There was no one in there, though. There was no one in the house except for me and Christine.

I went back into the living room and sat back down on the couch. I felt like such an idiot. "This place is just old," I said. "Those noises are probably just the house settling."

I looked at Christine. She was as white as a ghost.

Goddamnit, I thought. What are you doing to this poor girl?

14

I decided never to drive Pablo again after the night I'd thought we were getting home invaded. I made the decision quickly, the moment that I woke up in the morning. Even though I was still kind of surprised at what Pablo had done to his customers, I had to accept it. The guy was a scumbag. I decided that I just wasn't going to deal with someone like that, who ripped people off. I wasn't going to deal with any crack dealers anymore, for that matter. "I'm done with this shit," I told myself, as I stood on the balcony, having a smoke. "I'm done smoking crack, man."

That morning, after I took Christine to school, I called up Pablo to tell him that I wasn't going to drive him around anymore. I also wanted to get my digital scale back from him, assuming that he still had it. I was starting to wonder if maybe he'd already sold it for crack or something on Saturday night, when he'd fallen in.

"I still have your scale," Pablo told me. "But will you please explain to me what's going on here, Jim? Why don't you want to be my driver anymore?"

"You know those customers that you ripped off on Saturday night?" I said.

"Huh? What are you talking about?"

"Don't play dumb with me, man. I know what you did, Pablo. One of the guys that you ripped off came at me last night with a knife. He told me everything. You sold him a fifty piece and when he got home, he found out that it was a piece of soap. I'm done with you, man. I don't need this fucking shit. Now where are you right now? Are you at home? I want to come by and get my digital scale."

Pablo started to tell me some bullshit story about how he could get me a better scale than the one that I had.

"What the hell are you talking about?" I said. "Do you even still have my scale?"

"Of course I do," Pablo said. "I told you that already."

"Then the one that I lent you will be fine. Where are you?"

Pablo gave me an address. It was a house in downtown Hamilton.

"You're in Hamilton this early?" I said. "I thought you'd be in Burlington."

"No, I haven't gone back there yet," Pablo said. "I've been here since I fell in."

"OK, all right. Don't go anywhere. I'll be right over."

I hung up the phone and drove over to the house that Pablo had told me to go to. A guy about Pablo's age answered the door. He looked totally baked. His eyes were bloodshot and the place reeked of weed.

"Where's Pablo at?" I said.

"Pablo?" the guy said. "I don't know, man. I haven't seen that mofo in a couple of days."

"Don't give me that bullshit. I just talked to him on the phone five minutes ago. He told me that he was hanging out here. Now where is he?"

The guy looked at me and shrugged. "I don't know what to tell you," he said. "I think you been played, bro."

I realized that the guy was telling the truth. Pablo had never been at this house.

"OK," I said. "Sorry to bother you."

I didn't hear from Pablo for the rest of the day. I tried calling him a couple of times because I still wanted to get my scale back if he had it, but he wouldn't answer his phone.

By the evening, I was jonesing pretty bad. I had money that I'd made at the Woodbine, so I went to Chester's and just bought myself some dope.

So much for quitting, I thought, as I drove over there.

After buying dope a few times, I ran out of money. On Tuesday night, I found myself jonesing again. I tried to get a hold of Pablo—I was willing to drive him again, under the circumstances—but he still wouldn't answer his phone.

I started to get really pissed off. Christine noticed this and asked me what was wrong.

"It's my weed guy," I said. "I lent him my digital scale— you know the one that I use for selling weed to the guys on the show in the summertime? Anyway, now I can't get a hold of him."

Christine kind of cringed when I mentioned the scale. She never liked that I sold weed on the show during the season. She didn't mind me smoking it, but selling it was another matter, especially when I already had two pot convictions. Christine knew that I only sold to people on the show, though, so she put up with it.

"I know the scale you're talking about," Christine said. "Why did you lend that to him, Jim? This guy's a weed dealer. Shouldn't he have his own scale?"

"He's got one, but mine's better," I said. "I told him that he could use it. Now I think that he just fucked off with it. I've been calling him all day, but he won't answer his phone."

Christine just shrugged and went back to her studying.

For a while, I sat in the living room, jonesing my ass off. I wanted to get high so badly that I started to think about going to Chester's to see if Chester or Sal could hook me up with another dealer who needed a driver. I decided not to do this, though. It just seemed like too much of a hassle. I just wanted to get my dope and get high. I didn't want to have to deal with any crack dealers or their bullshit.

I finally couldn't take it anymore. I decided to just ask Christine if she'd lend me sixty bucks.

"What do you need sixty bucks for?" Christine said.

"I want to get some weed," I said.

"I just gave you money for that a few days ago."

"I know, but I smoked it all already."

"I thought you said that you couldn't get a hold of your weed guy, though. How are you going to buy weed?"

"I'm going to go to Dave's weed guy."

Christine sighed. "All right," she said. "I'll give you sixty dollars. After this, that's it, though, OK? I don't want you to ask me for any more money. I can't afford this, Jim."

"Don't worry," I said. "I won't ask you again. I promise."

Christine put her coat on and we went down to the car. We drove over to the TD bank at Centre Mall and Christine took sixty dollars out of the bank machine.

As soon as Christine put the money into my hand, I

immediately felt better. I drove home, dropped her off outside our building, and then drove straight to Chester's.

In the morning I got up and drove Christine to school. I went home afterwards, took a nap, and then cleaned out my stem. When the buzz wore off, I tried calling up Pablo again. I still couldn't get a hold of him.

I kept trying Pablo throughout the day. At around eight o'clock at night, he finally answered his phone.

"What the hell do you want, Jim?" Pablo said. "This is starting to get annoying."

"I want you to give me back my digital scale," I said.

"Wow, you're really not going to stop bitching about that scale, are you?"

"Look, either you give it back to me, or I go over to your apartment in Burlington right now and wait for you in the parking lot. What's it going to be?"

"Is that a threat?"

"Correct."

"Hey, I know where you live, too, Jim. Why don't I just show up at your house right now and punch you in the head right in front of your girlfriend?"

Pablo was this skinny little punk-ass kid. I couldn't believe how fucking bold he was being with me.

"Go ahead," I said. "Bring it, you little shit. I'll be waiting for you on the street, in front of my building."

"OK," Pablo said. "See you in a few minutes."

I put the phone down and immediately searched for a weapon. If Pablo thought that he was going to punch me in the head, he had another thing coming. I wasn't just some kid that was scared of his threats. I was really going to beat his ass if I had to. What was he going to do about it anyway, call the cops? He was a crack dealer for fuck's sake.

I went over to my daughter's toy box, in the bedroom. I found a mini wooden baseball bat in there that Dave had given her one time when she was over for the weekend. It was perfect for beating someone in the kneecaps with. I grabbed it and headed for the door.

I was hoping to make a quick exit, but before I could leave, I got some static from Christine.

"What's with the bat?" Christine said.

"You know how I told you that I couldn't get a hold of my weed guy?" I said.

"Yeah."

"Well, I just got a hold of him. He said that he's going to give me back my digital scale. I'm going out right now to meet with him."

"And you need a baseball bat to do that?"

I tapped the end of the bat into the palm of my hand and squeezed it, imaging how good it would feel to bash Pablo in the kneecaps with it.

"I guess you can say that I don't trust this guy anymore," I said. "I'm thinking that he might try something. I just want to be prepared in case he does."

"Prepared for what?" Christine said.

"I don't know. You never know what a person might do, Christine. This guy ain't exactly all right in the head, if you catch my drift. The bat's just for intimidation. I don't think I'll really have to use it. I think that he'll just give me my scale back and that'll be that."

"What if he doesn't give you your scale back, though? What if he doesn't get intimidated when he sees the bat?"

"Well, I guess I'm going to have to fucking beat him in the kneecaps with it, then, won't I?"

Christine got really upset. "Jim!" she wailed.

"Oh, it'll be fine, baby," I said. "He'll probably see the bat and back down like a little bitch."

I went down to my car and drove around to the front of our building. I parked on the street and then got out and waited for Pablo. Even though the street was pretty quiet—everything on Ottawa was closed already except for some restaurants and a couple of convenience stores—I didn't want some random person to walk by and see me standing there with a baseball bat. To conceal the bat in my hand, I opened my passenger door and stood on the sidewalk, while pretending to fiddle with something on the passenger side of my car.

After about ten minutes, a car approached and pulled over across the street from where I was standing. The passenger door opened and Pablo got out. He started to walk briskly towards me.

I immediately slammed my passenger door closed, stepped out from behind my car, and swung the bat over my shoulder.

Pablo stopped dead in his tracks. He looked stunned. "What's with the bat?" he said.

"What do you think?" I said.

"You're not really going to hit me with that thing, are you?"

"Why don't you come over here and find out?"

Pablo didn't move.

"Not so tough now, are you?" I said. "On the phone you told me that you were going to punch me in the head, remember?"

"Look, Jim, I'm sorry," Pablo said. "Forget what I said on the phone, OK? I was just talking trash. Now put the fucking bat away. Jesus!"

I brought the bat down from over my shoulder. "OK, so where's my scale?" I said.

"I don't have it," Pablo said.

"Why not?"

"I sold it."

"All right. Let's talk compensation, then. And not just for the scale, by the way. I let you use it free of charge and then you turned around and tried to fucking screw me for it. I want to be compensated for your use of it, too."

"How's a hundred piece sound?"

"That sounds all right."

"OK, good. Are we cool now?"

"Yeah, we're cool. I'll tell you right now, though, Pablo, if you ever pull any shit like this with me again, I'm not going to be so fucking nice next time, all right? I'm actually going to use this thing on you. That's a promise."

Pablo nodded. "OK," he said. "I get it."

Once I'd worked things out with Pablo, I suddenly didn't feel too bad about driving him somewhere. "Do you need me to drive you anywhere tonight?" I said. "Or is that your new driver?"

Pablo glanced at the guy in the car across the street. "No," he said. "He just gave me a ride over here. I actually need to make a couple of deliveries. Do you mind driving me?"

"No problem," I said.

For the next couple of hours, I drove Pablo around while he made his deliveries. A few of the customers that Pablo sold to were ones that he'd ripped off. Pablo smoothed things over with all of them, just like Sal had said he would.

At midnight I dropped Pablo off in Burlington. He gave me the hundred piece that he'd promised me, plus what he owed me for driving him.

I drove home. Christine came right to the door.

"Did you work everything out with that guy?" Christine said.

"Yeah," I said. "Everything's fine now."

15

A few days after I'd worked things out with Pablo, I went back to work at the Woodbine with Dave. It was now the last weekend in March. The mall, as usual, was pretty busy. I managed to walk out of there again with over three hundred bucks.

Each night after work, I bought dope off Pablo. When I was done smoking, I called Pablo up again and bought more. I didn't really trust Pablo anymore, so I always had my baseball bat with me whenever I had to deal with him—the Automatic Goof Beater, I called it. I kept it at arm's reach at all times. I wanted to make sure that Pablo really understood that I wasn't playing around with him; that I would seriously beat him if he ever pulled any shit with me again.

On Monday morning, while Christine got ready for school, I went downstairs to see if my welfare cheque had arrived. I'd been expecting it since Friday. If you weren't receiving direct deposits from welfare, you usually received your cheque in the mail on the third last business day of the month, which in this case would have been Friday, March 27.

All of our mail and the downstairs neighbours' mail got delivered through a slot in the street door. I went down to the street door, picked up the mail from off the ground, and looked through it. There were some flyers and a letter for the neighbours that looked important, but that was it. No welfare cheque.

What the hell? I thought. Where's my damn cheque?

I started to get worried. I tossed the mail onto the ground and went back upstairs to the apartment.

In the apartment, Christine was in the kitchen, getting her lunch ready. She was standing at the counter, spreading peanut butter onto a piece of bread.

Christine noticed the worried look on my face. "What's wrong?" she said.

"My welfare cheque didn't come yet," I said.

"Shouldn't you have gotten it by now?"

"Yeah."

"That's weird. Why do you think it hasn't come yet?"

"I don't know. I think I'm going to have to go to welfare today and ask them about it."

I went down to the car and had a smoke while I waited for Christine. Ten minutes later, Christine came down. We got on the road and headed over to the university.

After I'd dropped Christine off, I went over to the welfare office. I went up to the desk and told the secretary that I hadn't received my welfare cheque yet and that I needed to speak to Theresa, my worker.

"She's currently with another client right now," the

secretary told me. "If you'll just have a seat, sir, she'll be with you in a moment."

I sat down next to some pamphlets and waited.

About fifteen minutes later, Theresa came out of her office and into the waiting area. She smiled at me. "Hi, Jim," she said. "Let's go to my office."

Theresa led me down a hallway to her office. It was a small room with no windows.

"What can I do for you today?" Theresa said, as she sat down at her desk.

"I haven't got my cheque yet," I said. "You guys were supposed to mail it to me."

Theresa typed something into her computer at lightning speed. "According to our records, your cheque was mailed out on . . . the twenty-fifth of March. You should have received it by now."

"Well, I didn't get it."

"You haven't moved recently, have you?"

"No, I haven't moved. I'm still on Ottawa Street."

Theresa typed some more information into her computer.

"So, what happens now?" I said. "Are you guys going to give me another cheque?"

"Well, no," Theresa said. "Your cheque has already been released. We can't release another one to you at this time. What I'd suggest is that you wait a few more days while we look into this on our end. In all likelihood, Jim, you'll get it in the mail in a day or two."

"What if I don't get it?"

"You probably will."

I left the welfare office and went over to Dave's. It was only around ten o'clock in the morning, but Dave was already in the middle of a poker tournament.

Dave and I smoked a joint and talked, while Dave continued to play poker. I was just about to tell him what had happened with welfare when he started complaining to me about Belinda, who wasn't home.

"You know what she did to me the other day, man?" Dave said.

"What?" I said.

"She ditched me."

"What do you mean, she ditched you?"

"We were in the car, arguing about something. We stopped at the liquor store over at Eastgate Square and I went in to get her some Mike's Hard Lemonade. While I was in the store, she drove off. I waited for a while, but she didn't come back. I had to take the bus home."

"Yeah, well you think you've got problems. I just got back from welfare."

"Oh, yeah, what happened? Did you miss one of those stupid employment meetings or something?"

"No, I haven't got my cheque yet."

"Really? I got mine on Friday."

"That's great, Dave. Good for you."

"What did welfare say about it?

"They told me to wait. They think that it's still in the mail."

Dave's computer beeped. "Cock soup!" he said.

"What?" I said.

"This prick keeps going all in."

Dave clicked the mouse next to his laptop. He folded his hand and then took a big haul off the joint we were smoking. He coughed so hard that his face turned as red as a ripe tomato.

"You know, I wouldn't be surprised if your cheque was ripped off," Dave said, once he'd stopped coughing. "If they mailed it out when they were supposed to, you should have gotten it by now."

Even though I didn't like hearing this, I was already thinking it myself. "Yeah, I'm starting to think that, too," I said.

Dave sat out the next couple of hands of his poker tournament. He was now giving me his full attention.

"Who do you think might have stolen your cheque?" Dave said.

"I don't know," I said. "Probably my downstairs neighbours. All of our mail gets shoved through the same slot in the street door. It might have even been one of the neighbours' friends who did it. Who knows? They're constantly having people over. How hard is it to grab a piece of mail off the ground, you know?"

"Buddy downstairs just got home invaded," Dave said, now that we were on the subject of neighbours.

"Imagine that," I said.

"Yeah, he got beat up pretty bad. I heard that it was his friends that did it. He ripped them off or something and then they came back and retaliated."

"What are you trying to say?" I said. "That I should go down there and break my neighbours' kneecaps? Do a home invasion? Serves you right for stealing my mail?"

Dave started to laugh. "Oh, fuck yeah!" he said.

I suddenly thought of my baseball bat and the night that I'd nearly used it on Pablo. Dave never heard that little story. That's because I'd never told Dave that I'd been smoking crack all winter and driving around crack dealers. Somehow, though, I'm sure that he knew. There wasn't much that got by Dave. He was a carny. He'd been there, done that, got the t-shirt. Now it was all about poker.

Dave settled down.

"You got Neil's number?" I said.

Neil was a guy from the show who ran a moving company in Toronto. It was a shitty little operation that barely made any money, except for around the first of the month, when most people who rented moved.

"Yeah, I've got it," Dave said. "Why?"

"Because it's the end of the month, man," I said. "Maybe he's got some work. If I don't make some money in the next couple of days, I'm going to be fucked for my half of April rent and my car insurance."

"OK, I'll call him."

16

Dave called Neil and got some work lined up for us at the moving company the next day. Since the moving company was in Toronto, we had to get up at the crack of dawn to get there by seven o'clock in the morning. I could get up no problem, but I was worried about Dave. I called him at five thirty the next morning to make sure that he was up.

Dave answered the phone on the fourth or fifth ring. He groaned and then hacked a couple of times. They were the nasty, phlegmy hacks of a guy who'd been smoking two packs a day for the last twenty years of his life and was just waking up. "Ugh," Dave said. "Too tired, man . . . up late last night . . . won fifty bucks."

I pulled the phone away from my ear and literally scowled at it for a second. "I don't want to hear any of your excuses, Dave," I said. "Just get your ass out of bed and get down to the car. We're leaving in half an hour."

"OK, fine," Dave said. "I'll get ready."

At six o'clock, Dave came down to the car. We jumped on the QEW and drove to Toronto. Because the roads were dry and we'd left early, we were able to beat the morning rush.

When we got to the moving company, we met with Neil's wife, Patty. After some small talk, Patty led us out to where the trucks were parked. Patty told us where the first job was and gave me the keys to the truck since Dave didn't drive.

It turned out that there was a lot of waiting around between jobs that day. The jobs that we did get were backbreaking and the money sucked. I drove the truck and did the paperwork, so I made fifteen bucks an hour, plus whatever I got in tips. Dave only made ten bucks an hour, plus tips.

If the waiting around between jobs wasn't bad enough, the customers were especially awful. One customer, some cheap-ass paki, started haggling with me about the bill at the end of the job.

I tried to explain to the guy where the extra fees were coming from. "It's an extra hundred dollars because you weren't packed and ready to go when we got here," I said.

"Vhat you talking 'bout?" buddy yelled. "Vee ver ready!"

I wanted to smack him in the head with the fucking clipboard.

In the afternoon there was nothing was going on for a couple of hours, so Dave and I decided to break for lunch.

"Let's go get some dirty bird," Dave said. "It's Toonie Tuesday."

"I don't know where the KFC is around here," I said. "Why don't we just go to McDonald's? There's one right up the street."

"I don't feel like McDonald's. I want KFC."

Dave made a point of making me use the GPS from the moving truck to find out where the nearest KFC was. I could have just told him to suck it. Dave could barely figure out his computer, never mind use a GPS. I went along with it, though, because Dave was my friend. I only started to regret the decision after we got to the KFC and I had to sit there, in the parking lot, and watch Dave lick grease off his disgusting fingers.

Just when it was starting to look bleak, Dave and I scored on our last job of the day: two rich gay guys moving into a brand new condo on Spadina Avenue, near the Gardiner Expressway. The condo was the size of a fucking closet, but rich people are willing to pay big bucks, it turns out, to live in a tiny box next to a freeway and hear cars and trucks roaring by their bedroom window first thing in the morning.

Once we'd gotten all of the gay guys' stuff off the truck and into their apartment, there wasn't enough room for all their stuff. The place we'd moved them out of had been a lot bigger.

The gay guys wanted us to move some of their stuff downstairs to a storage locker in their building. Because of a delay we'd had with the service elevator, though, it was getting late and we had to get back to the moving company.

"If you come back tomorrow, we'll make it worth your while," the gay guys told us. "How's fifty bucks each in cash sound?"

The stuff that the gay guys wanted us to move would have only taken a couple of trips in the service elevator. And since we didn't need the moving truck, we wouldn't need to involve the moving company. I figured that we'd have some time to kill between moving jobs, so I knew that we'd be able to do it. It would have been crazy to pass up fifty bucks each for that little amount of work.

"OK," I said. "We'll call you tomorrow when we have an opening in our schedule."

We left the gay guys' place and went back to the moving company. I dropped off the truck, returned the keys to Patty, and then Patty paid me and Dave under the table, in cash. With all the gaps we'd had in the schedule that day, I ended up getting paid for only nine hours of work, which worked out to a hundred and thirty-five bucks. With tips, I ended up making about two hundred, but that was only because the gay gays had given Dave and I each a really good tip.

By the time Dave and I got back to Hamilton that night, it was almost eleven o'clock. My plan had been to drop Dave off and then call up Pablo. When we got home, though, we found two cop cars parked on Ottawa Street, outside my building.

I parked the car as fast as I could and then ran up the wooden staircase, two steps at a time, to my apartment. When I got to the top of the stairs, I flung the stairwell door open and found a broad cop. She was standing on the landing outside the downstairs neighbours' door.

"What's going on down there?" I asked the cop.

The cop's radio squawked. The sound bounced off the walls of the stairwell.

"We're responding to a domestic call, sir," the cop said. "Everything is under control now. We'll be clearing out soon."

I put my key in my door, relieved that it was still locked and on its hinges, and went into my apartment.

Christine came to the door. She was totally shaken. She

started rambling to me about what happened.

"I felt like such a jerk calling the cops," Christine said. "She was screaming so loud, though, it sounded like he was killing her. The 911 operator asked me if there were any children living downstairs and what my name was. I didn't give her my name. Just as I was giving her directions on how to get here, she told me that a message had popped up on her screen, telling her that someone else had already called 911 and that some officers were on their way over."

As Christine was telling all of this to me, we suddenly heard a loud thud, like a scuffle had been going on downstairs and someone had just gotten tackled to the ground. Christine nearly jumped ten feet in the air.

I reached into my pocket and gave Christine a hundred and twenty dollars.

"What's this for?" Christine said.

"It's for the rent," I said.

Christine took the money. She was still in such a daze, though, that she didn't even bother to count it.

"I'll give you more tomorrow," I said. "Dave and I have some more moving jobs lined up. By the way, did my welfare cheque come today?"

"No," Christine said.

The cursor blinked in the middle of Christine's computer screen. I looked at the stats textbook and the coffee cup sitting there, on the end table, and realized that these were all the signs of another all-nighter that was about to occur.

Better to just leave her alone so that she can get some work done, I thought, and headed for the door.

"Dave wants me to drive him to his weed guy's house right now," I said. "I just came home to let you know that I was done work, and to give you that money, and then I saw the cop cars, so I came upstairs."

Christine had too much on her mind at that moment to care about my bullshit excuses. The night would soon be turning into the next morning and she still had her stats assignment to finish.

"That's fine, honey," Christine said. "You go ahead."

I left the house and called up Pablo. He was still in downtown Hamilton. I met him at a crack house, bought a forty piece off him, and then went straight home to get high.

By the time that I was done getting high, and had come down enough to sleep, it was two thirty in the morning. I slept for three hours and then got up and called Dave.

"Ugh," Dave groaned, when he finally answered the phone. "Too tired, man . . . up late last night again . . . won another fifty bucks."

Not this shit again, I thought.

It was like a scene straight out of *Groundhog Day*, that old movie with Bill Murray, where he keeps re-living the same day over and over again. Only instead of Sonny and Cher on the radio, I had Dave groaning into the phone, telling me that he was too tired to go to work because he stupidly stayed up most of the night again, playing poker. I'd stayed up late, too, smoking crack, but at least I was able to get up in the morning. What was Dave's excuse? It wasn't like he'd been high out of his mind or something. He'd been with it enough to know that he should stop playing poker and go to bed.

"Dave, you can sleep in the car on the way over there," I said.

Dave groaned some more. That was his response: more groaning.

I thought of Bill Murray. Where the fuck was the toaster? I wondered. I wanted to throw it into the bathtub with me to see if I'd get a chance at a new day.

I hung up the phone and turned to Christine. She was still up, working on the stats assignment she had to finish.

"What's the matter?" Christine said.

"Dave doesn't want to go to work," I said.

"Why not?"

"He was up all night playing poker."

Christine rolled her eyes. They were bloodshot from staring at the computer screen all night. "What's new?" she said. "Are you still going?"

"Yeah, we need the money," I said. "I just hope I don't end up going there for nothing now, though. I don't know if the moving company is going to have another mover to send out with me."

"Why don't you go downstairs and ask Marcus to go with you? Weren't you always taking him with you to the temp company back in the fall? He could probably use the work."

Yeah, the *work*, I thought.

What Christine didn't know about Marcus, the black guy who lived in our building, was that he was a crackhead. The only reason why he ever came upstairs to ask me if I'd take him to the temp company was because his wife, who an even bigger crackhead than he was, would get on his case and tell him to go make some money so that they could get high.

I realized what the situation with the black people was the first time that I met them, right after they moved in. Marcus invited me downstairs to their apartment and as soon as I got down there, his wife offered me a free hit of crack. You'd think that people are just being friendly, offering you a free blast like that, but really it's just to get you to come back fifteen minutes later, asking for more, so that they can run out and get it for you and get a tip in return.

I lied to the black people and told them straight-up that I didn't smoke crack. I'd been living in Hamilton for over a year at that point and had already met Chester. I didn't need anyone in my building to run out and get dope for me. I wasn't using that much at that time anyway. I was only doing a forty piece about once a month. Christine wasn't living with me yet, but she was visiting me a few days a week. The last thing I needed was to have the neighbour coming upstairs to my apartment while she was there, offering me dope. I felt that it was better getting my dope through Chester at that time anyway, even though I hated going over there and having to wait around in that nasty apartment. Crack dealers were always giving me their numbers when I bought dope with Chester, but I always threw them away because I knew that if it was more of a pain in the ass to get dope that I'd do it less often. It wasn't until a couple of months before my trip to Edmonton, when I started working temp jobs, that I stopped going to Chester's and started calling up an actual crack dealer. Somehow having to go to Chester's just wasn't enough of a deterrent for me anymore. Since I was buying dope every day after work anyway, I decided that I might as well just cut out the middleman and go straight to the source. The day that I left for Edmonton was the day that I told myself that I needed to quit. I was sick of getting high all the time, and I was sick of lying to Christine and being a financial burden on her. As I left the house to pick up my daughter, on the way to the airport, I deleted my dealer's number from my phone. At the time, I honestly thought that I was done with my crack habit. I knew that I'd be staying at my mom's house in Edmonton and that

I'd have my daughter with me twenty-four seven, so I knew that I wouldn't be able to go downtown and look for it.

I knew that Christine would have never suggested that I go to the moving company with Marcus if she knew that he was a crackhead. Christine wouldn't have wanted me to even associate with a person like that, given my history of crack use. But Christine didn't know this. I wasn't sure if Marcus would answer his door so early in the morning, but I went down there and knocked on it anyway.

I had to knock about ten times, but Marcus eventually answered his door.

"Jim, what the hell?" Marcus said, as he stood there, rubbing his eyes, still half asleep.

"Sorry to wake you up," I said. "I've got good news for you, though, buddy. I've got some work for you today. Are you up for it?"

Marcus hesitated. "What kind of work?" he said.

"Some moving jobs," I said. "Some customers promised me and my buddy fifty bucks each in cash if we came back today to move some stuff into a storage locker in their condo. My buddy flaked out on me. If you come to work with me today, you'll get the fifty bucks. The other jobs will be ten bucks an hour, plus tips."

"Are these jobs in Hamilton?"

"No, Toronto."

"A'ight," Marcus said. "Just let me go talk to my wife."

After talking to his wife, Marcus came down to the car and we drove to Toronto. We went straight to the moving company and checked in with Patty.

"Dave ain't feeling well today so I brought my neighbour with me," I told Patty. "I hope that's OK."

"Is he a good mover?" Patty said.

"Oh, you bet," I said.

That was good enough for Patty.

"OK, well, the job that I have you guys scheduled for doesn't start until ten o'clock," Patty said. "Maybe you guys want to go get a coffee or something."

Seeing as how we had a lot of time to kill, I called up the gay guys and told them that we had an opening in our schedule.

"OK," the gay guys said. "Come on over."

Marcus and I got into my car and we drove over to the gay guys' place. We moved their stuff into their storage locker, and then they gave us each fifty bucks in cash, as promised.

While we were on our way back to the moving company, Patty called me on my cell phone. "Hey, I need you to drive over to this house," she said. "This woman needs her couch thrown out."

"What do you mean, thrown out?" I said. "Just take it to the curb?"

"Yeah, she just wants us to chuck it for her."

Patty gave me the broad's address. It was a house off Yonge and Lawrence.

When we got to the house, I couldn't believe the couch that the broad wanted thrown out. It was in perfect condition. It was a rich neighbourhood, though, so I shouldn't have been all that shocked.

We chucked the couch and then went back to the moving company.

"You know that job that's supposed to start at ten o'clock?" Patty told us when we got there.

"Yeah," I said.

"Well, it got cancelled. I'm sorry, guys. I've got another one, but it doesn't start until four."

There was so much time until the next job that we

decided to go back to Hamilton for a while.

Christine had already left for school when I got home, so I sat down on the couch and put on a show that I'd downloaded. I set the alarm clock on my phone just in case I fell asleep, which turned out to be a good idea because as soon as I got comfortable, my eyelids started to get heavy and within a few minutes, I passed right out.

At a quarter to two, the alarm clock went off. I went downstairs to Marcus' apartment, feeling groggy and shitty, and knocked on the door.

I knocked for a while, but nobody answered.

"Un-fucking-believable," I muttered.

I suddenly lost all motivation to go back to Toronto for the four o'clock moving job.

Fuck it, I thought. There may not be any point.

I decided to just call up Pablo and drive him around instead.

17

A couple of days after I went to the moving company with Marcus, I got a call from Theresa, my worker.

"I'd like you to come in today," Theresa said. "I need to talk to you about your cheque."

It was Friday morning and I still hadn't gotten my welfare cheque in the mail. I was wondering if welfare was finally going to release another one to me.

Theresa wouldn't confirm anything over the phone. "We'll discuss that when you come in," she said.

I immediately left the house and drove over to the welfare office.

When I got over to welfare, Theresa led me to her office. She immediately produced a piece of paper. "Please take a look at this," she said.

I looked at the piece of paper. It was a photocopy of my welfare cheque—the one that had been mailed out to me on the twenty-fifth of March. It was stamped, indicating that it had been cashed. The place where it had been cashed was some little store.

"When did you find out about this?" I said.

"This morning," Theresa said.

I looked at the signature on the back of the cheque. It was nothing like my signature. The person who endorsed the thing obviously had no idea that I never wrote out my entire last name when I signed my name, or that my handwriting looked like a Grade 3 kid's chicken scratch, not like the perfectly written John Hancock displayed there in front of me.

"I guess you can see that this clearly ain't my signature," I said.

"Yes," Theresa said. "That's why I asked you to come in."

Theresa put the piece of paper into a folder on her desk. Then she pulled out another piece of paper. She handed it to me. It was an affidavit.

After reviewing the form with me, Theresa asked me to fill it out and sign it. "We'll be forwarding this onto the fraud department," she told me. "They'll be able to determine where the pressure points are in your signature and then compare it to the ones on the cheque."

"Listen," I said, as I printed my name at the top of the form. "You really don't need to conduct an investigation into this, OK? I can tell you right now who stole it, or at least give you a pretty good idea."

"That might be so, but we still have to act in accordance with the law," Theresa said. "I can assure you that a thorough investigation will be conducted into this matter, Jim. Cashing a stolen cheque is a very serious offence."

I wrote a brief statement and then signed and dated the form.

I handed the form back to Theresa. "What happens now?" I said. "Do I get another cheque?"

"No, not yet," Theresa said.

After having sat there and obediently signed the necessary paperwork, I was astounded at what Theresa was now telling me. "But you already know that my cheque was stolen," I said. "That's why you had me sign this thing, right? Why can't you just give me another cheque?"

"I'm afraid that we can't release another cheque to you until fraud conducts an investigation," Theresa said.

"How long is that going to take?"

"We should hear something pretty soon."

I shook my head in disbelief.

The next thing I knew, Theresa was handing me yet another piece of paper. This one had a list of food banks on it with their addresses and hours of operation.

How humiliating, I thought.

"What about my rent?" I said. "It's past due."

Theresa looked at me warmly. "You should talk to your landlord," she said. "Hopefully, you can work something out until we hear back from fraud."

I took the list of food banks from Theresa and quickly left the welfare office. When I got home about ten minutes later, I told Christine what happened.

"You mean to tell me that somebody stole your cheque and welfare refused to give you another one?" Christine said. "What kind of bullshit is that?"

"They said that the fraud department needs to look into it first," I said.

Christine sighed and shook her head. "That's unbelievable," she said.

About an hour after getting home from the welfare office, I went out to drive Pablo. When I got home later that afternoon, Christine was studying. I went into the bathroom and got high.

Once the high had worn off and I was ready to drive Pablo again, Christine asked me if I'd take her grocery shopping. I really wasn't in the mood to go shopping. I wanted to go drive Pablo again so that I could get some more dope.

"Can we do that later?" I said. "I don't really feel like going to No Frills right now."

"Come on, Jim," Christine said. "There's almost no food left in the fridge."

I wanted to avoid an argument, so I took Christine to the grocery store. When we got home, we just so happened to run into the Native guy who lived downstairs.

"You go on upstairs," I told to Christine, as we were coming around the corner with the groceries. "I'll be up in a second."

The minute that Christine was out of sight, I set the groceries down on the sidewalk, so that they were out of the way, and then walked over to the neighbour. He was standing at the bus stop, having a smoke and talking to some guy. The guy was wearing a jean jacket and a pair of dirty, beige shorts, even though it was only a few degrees outside. He had a case of Molson Canadian on the sidewalk, at his feet.

As soon as the guy with the beer saw me coming, he scooped up the beer and then crossed the street.

I went up to the neighbour and got right up in his face.

"Can I help you?" the neighbour said.

"Yeah, I had some mail that went missing," I said. "I'm wondering if you might have seen it. It was from Ontario Works."

"Sorry, I didn't see any mail like that."

The neighbour took a drag off his smoke and then turned away from me.

"OK, let's try this again," I said. "My welfare cheque was sent here last week. It was stolen and cashed. You got any idea about who might have done that?"

"Are you asking me if I stole it?" the neighbour said.

"You know damn right I am! It was either you, or one of your friends. So, tell me, which one of you guys fucking did it?"

The neighbour took a step towards me and puffed out his chest. "Who the fuck do you think you are?" he said. "Do you want me to beat the shit out of you, right here on the sidewalk?"

The neighbour was this old fucker. His arm was all bandaged up like he'd just gotten out of the hospital.

I glanced down at the neighbour's arm and literally laughed. "You're going to beat the shit out of me?" I said. "You look like you just got out of the hospital, old man. Is that what happened to you the other night, when you and your old lady were scrapping and the cops had to come here? It looks like she fucked your arm up pretty good. But, hey, I got a baseball bat. I can fuck your other arm up for you, too, if you want. The bat's in my car. Hold on a sec. I'll go get it."

I left the neighbour to contemplate the idea of having two fucked up arms, while I went to my car to get my bat.

When I got back a minute later, the neighbour was gone. Feeling disappointed, I picked up the groceries that I'd left on the sidewalk and went upstairs to the apartment.

Christine was in the kitchen, still putting away groceries when I got in the door.

"What were you doing down there for so long?" Christine said.

"Just talking to the neighbour," I said.

Christine stopped putting away the groceries. She looked at me and noticed the bat in my hand. She immediately put her hand on her hip.

"What?" I said.

"What did you say to him, Jim? I hope you're not going to get into some kind of feud or whatever with the neighbours now over this welfare cheque thing."

"Oh, you bet I am!" I said. "They ripped us off, Christine. We can't let them think that they can get away with that shit. I just let the neighbour know that he should watch his back from now on, that's all. I think he got the message."

My phone rang. It was Pablo.

I told Pablo that I'd pick him up, and then hung up the phone.

"I've got to get going now, baby," I said to Christine. "Don't answer the door to anyone, OK? If it's me and I want you to open the door, I'll knock like this."

I knocked on the door to demonstrate. Christine looked totally freaked out.

"Love you," I said.

I grabbed my baseball bat, gave Christine a kiss, and then headed out the door.

18

Pablo had been hanging out at a crack house downtown, while I'd been home, on my break. I drove over there, picked him up, and then drove him around while he made some deliveries.

One of the deliveries that Pablo made was to Sal. We met him at the Tim Hortons on Barton Street, next to the Esso gas station.

"Hey, Pablo," Sal said, as he got into the car. "The cops are looking for you, man."

"Oh, yeah?" Pablo said.

"Yeah. This red Chrysler minivan showed up here just a few minutes ago. Two plainclothes cops got out and jacked me up. The one cop asked for you by name. 'You seen Pablo?' he said. Those were his exact words."

"Did they say anything else?"

"No, they just wanted to know if I seen you around."

"What'd you tell them?"

"What do you think I told them? I told them to get fucked!"

Pablo nodded. "OK, Sal," he said. "Thanks for the tip."

Pablo gave Sal his piece and we got back on the road.

Like right before Bruce got busted, I suddenly got a bad feeling. "Hey, I think you should go back to Burlington," I told Pablo. "Wait a couple of days, man. Come back to Hamilton when the heat's off."

"Are you serious?" Pablo said.

"Yeah, I've got a bad feeling."

Pablo wasn't convinced. He didn't care about my bad feeling. "Jim, if the cops really wanted to bust me, don't you think that they'd just come out and bust me?" he said. "Why jack up some crackhead who they know is going to run straight to the dealer and tip him off?"

"Whatever, it's your call, man," I said. "Just make sure that your shit's on you, OK? I don't want any dope in my car if we end up getting jacked up."

"We're not going to get jacked up."

"Just do it."

"All right, it's on me. When the hell do I ever leave my shit in your car anyway?"

For the next forty-five minutes, I drove Pablo around and he made some more deliveries. Pablo seemed relaxed, joking around with the customers and shit, but I couldn't get what Sal had told us out of my head. The whole time that I drove, all I could think about were red Chrysler minivans and how I'd never noticed before how many people fucking had one. I kept seeing them everywhere, at every light, on every corner. I was starting to feel paranoid.

We ended up back on Barton Street, heading towards Centre Mall.

"I want to get a coffee," Pablo said all of a sudden. "Let's stop at Tim Hortons."

I pulled into the first Tim Hortons that we came to. It was the same one that we'd met Sal at earlier.

"Want anything?" Pablo said, as he got out of the car.

"No, I'm good," I said.

Pablo closed the door and walked off towards the store. I watched him in my rearview mirror for a second and then turned my attention back to the street. I was parked facing Barton. I watched the cars drive by as I sat there and waited.

After a few minutes, I started to get impatient. I started sneaking glances at Pablo through the store window every ten or twenty seconds to see if he was advancing in the line. Every time that I looked, though, there was still someone in front of him.

"Come on, man," I muttered. "Hurry up."

Suddenly, out of nowhere, two vehicles came barreling into the Tim Hortons parking lot and slammed on the brakes. One of the vehicles was a black Toyota Corolla. The other was a red Chrysler minivan.

Oh, shit, I thought. It's the cops.

The doors of the minivan flew open and two plainclothes cops jumped out and rushed towards the Tim Hortons. In my rearview mirror, I watched the cops burst into the store, make a beeline for Pablo, and tackle him to the ground. The people in the store were horrified. They were screaming and freaking out.

A few seconds later, the cops in the Toyota got out and came over to my car. One of the cops was young; the other was older. They both looked like your typical Hamilton cops, though. They were both about six foot two and built like CFL linebackers.

The older cop came up to my window. "License and registration, please," he said.

I reached into my pocket and pulled out my wallet. I took out my license and registration and handed them to the cop.

The cop looked at my license for a second and then looked at me. "Please step out of the vehicle, sir," he said.

"Why?" I said.

"We have probable cause to search this car."

I got out of my car.

"I'm going to need you to open the trunk now," the cop said.

"OK, but there ain't nothing in there," I said.

The cop didn't care. He had me open it anyway. My trunk didn't have a release button, so I actually had to get out and open it manually.

After inspecting the trunk, the older cop had the younger cop search the rest of my car.

While the younger cop was searching the driver's seat, he found something. "Hey, Les," he yelled, suddenly. "Check this out!"

In the younger cop's hand was the Automatic Goof Beater, my mini baseball bat. He was hoisting it up in the air like a goddamn trophy.

Les looked at the bat in the younger cop's hand. "Good work, Frank," he said. Then he turned to me and smirked. "What is it, baseball season already?" he said.

"Yup," I said.

A few minutes later, the cops were finished searching my car. It was obvious from the way that they were acting that they'd found absolutely nothing of interest in it.

"So, what's the score here?" I said. "Did you guys find anything? Am I free to go?"

"Just hold on a second," Les said.

"Why? Am I under arrest?"

"No."

"Then what do I need to stick around here for?"

"We've got some questions that we want to ask you."

I really didn't feel like answering any of the cops' questions. I knew that, legally, I didn't have to tell them anything.

I told the cops that I wasn't interested in talking to them, but they were persistent.

"It'll only take a couple of minutes," Frank, the younger cop, said. "We just want to ask you a couple of things about Pablo. After that, you can go on your way."

"But there's nothing to talk about," I said. "I hardly know the guy. I was just giving him a ride somewhere when you guys jacked me up."

Les wasn't buying it. "Don't give us that bullshit," he said. "We know that you know that Pablo is a crack dealer. I'm guessing that you're, what, driving him around to support your crack habit or something?"

"Look, man," I said. "You can think whatever you want. I don't have to talk to you guys. I'm out of here."

I turned and started to get into my car.

Suddenly, Les spoke up. "OK, Jim," he said. "You don't have to talk to us if you don't want to. That's fine. Maybe we'll just go over to your house later and talk to your wife, or your girlfriend. I'm sure that she knows a thing or two about what you've been up to. I'm sure that she'll be more willing to cooperate with us."

I was stunned. I couldn't believe how far the cops were willing to go just to get some fucking information out of me. They might have just been bluffing, of course, but I had no way of knowing this. They seemed like total dirtbags. I didn't put it past either one of them to actually go over to my house and do a thing like that. All I knew was that if the cops showed up at my house and talked to Christine, Christine would find out that I'd been driving around a crack dealer and then I'd be fucked. I'd have to tell her everything. I couldn't let the cops put me in that situation.

I knew that I was cornered. I told the cops that I'd talk to them later, reassuring them that there was no need to involve my girlfriend. The cops wanted to talk to me right then and there, though, at the Tim Hortons.

"I'll talk to you guys, just not here," I said. "Look at how much attention we're attracting. Some person walking by might recognize me. I don't want anyone to think that I'm giving information to the cops."

Les reached for his phone. "OK," he said. "We'll meet up somewhere later, then. What's your phone number?"

I gave Les my cell phone number. Les entered it into his phone.

In a couple of minutes, the cops cleared out from the Tim Hortons. I waited until they were long gone and then went over to Chester's. I didn't have much money on me. I'd spent almost everything I'd made at the Woodbine and the moving company on crack, except for the money I'd given Christine to put towards the rent. I had enough for a fifty piece, though. After dealing with the cops, I was desperate to get high.

As soon as I got to Chester's, I told Chester and Sal what happened to Pablo. I even told them about the cops and how they'd tried to get me to talk.

"Did you talk to them?" Chester said.

"Of course not," I said.

"Man, I can't believe it happened right at the same Tim

Hortons," Sal said. "What the hell did you guys go back there for? I told you that the cops had shown up there and that they were looking for Pablo."

"Yeah, that's pretty bad," Chester said. "You should have told that kid to get his ass back to Burlington and to lay low for a couple of days."

"I did tell him that," I said. "He wouldn't listen to me."

"Wow, what a fucking idiot," Sal said.

After waiting around for about twenty minutes, I went with Chester to meet the dealer.

By the time I got my dope and dropped Chester off, I wanted to get high so badly that I almost shit my pants before I got in the door.

19

The day after Pablo got busted, I went back to work at the Woodbine. I wasn't really in the mood to go there after everything that had happened the night before, but I knew that I'd make good money there again and I was broke.

As I was getting ready for work that morning, the downstairs neighbour came upstairs and knocked on my door.

"Hey, sorry to bother you so early in the morning," the neighbour said. "I just wanted to apologize for what happened yesterday. I was in a bad mood. I'm really sorry about your mail that went missing. I honestly don't know what happened to it."

I knew that the neighbour was lying to me through his teeth. He was only apologizing because he was old and injured and because it must have sunken in how badly I could beat him if I wanted to. I realized, however, that there was no point in continuing to feud with the guy. It wasn't like it would get me my welfare cheque back.

"It's OK," I said. "It was a misunderstanding."

I glanced down at the neighbour's arm. He still had that big bandage on it.

"You're probably wondering what happened to my arm," the neighbour said.

I didn't really care, but I asked him what happened.

"My girlfriend stabbed me," the neighbour said. "The other night, when we were fighting, she came at me with a kitchen knife. We were both pretty hammered. She didn't know what she was doing."

The neighbour offered me a smoke. I took one.

"I've got to get ready for work now," I said.

"All right," the neighbour said. "Talk to you later."

The neighbour went back downstairs to his apartment. I closed the door and went into the living room. Christine had just gotten up to use the bathroom.

"Who was that at the door?" Christine said.

"The downstairs neighbour," I said.

Christine eyes widened. She looked petrified.

"Don't worry," I said. "He just came up here to apologize."

I finished getting ready for work, and then drove to the Woodbine with Dave.

That night, after Dave and I finished work and we were leaving Toronto, we stopped at a Petro-Canada to fill up. Dave pitched in a couple of bucks for gas. He waited in the car, while I went inside to go pay.

A few minutes later, when I came back to the car, Dave had this weird look on his face.

"What?" I said. "What are you looking at me like that for?"

"This is going to sound kind of weird," Dave said. "But do you happen to have a CB radio in your car?"

I wasn't in any mood to play around. "Yeah, that does sound weird," I said. "No, Dave, I do not have a fucking CB in my car."

Before Dave could say anything else, I heard a noise suddenly. It was a noise like a CB makes when someone presses the button without talking.

"*That*," Dave said. "Did you hear that?"

"Yeah, I heard it," I said.

"What is that? I heard it earlier today, actually, but I thought that it was just another radio station cutting in."

"I have no idea."

We searched the car right there at the gas station. Within a couple of minutes, we found the source of the noise. It was coming from a walkie phone—a phone like they use in warehouses with a two-way radio built into it. The thing had been under Dave's seat.

As soon as I saw the phone, I knew exactly who it belonged to: it was the cops'. It was identical to the one that Les had—the one that he'd pulled out and entered my phone number into. Only I'd seen Les leave with his phone. This one had to belong to the younger cop, the one who'd searched my car.

I decided to be straight-up with Dave about the phone. "It's a cop's phone," I said.

"What do you have a cop's phone in your car for?" Dave said.

"Because I've been driving around crack dealers all winter. The guy that I was driving got busted last night. One of the cops forgot it when he searched my car."

Dave didn't look all that shocked. "Yeah, I thought that I saw a kid who looked like a crack dealer going to your place one time in the afternoon," he said. "Then another time, when I was over there, I thought I smelled it. Does Christine know what you've been doing?"

"What do you think?" I said.

We started to talk about what I should do with the phone. Dave had this fucked up idea that I should keep it.

"Why the hell would I want to do that?" I said.

"You could listen in on all of the cops' conversations and sell the information to dealers," Dave said. He started to laugh.

Go ahead and laugh, I thought. At least one of us thinks this is funny.

"Dave, the phone's probably got GPS," I said. "There's no way that I can keep it."

"If it's got GPS, why haven't the cops come back for it yet?" Dave said.

It was a really good question. I had to think about it for a few seconds.

"I don't know," I said. "Maybe the cop who forgot it is just too embarrassed to come back and get it himself. Maybe he's waiting for me to find it and give it back to him."

"What if he left it in your car on purpose?" Dave said. "You know, so that he could track your ass."

"Don't be ridiculous, man. You really think that a cop would leave his phone in someone's car on purpose with the volume turned up? It was only a matter of time before I found it."

I wanted to get rid of the cop's phone that night, but by the time we got back to Hamilton I was too stressed out and tired to bother doing this. Instead, I went over to Dave's house and smoked a joint with him.

After leaving Dave's, I wanted to get some dope. I didn't

want to go over to Chester's, though, with the cop's phone in my car, just in case the cops were actually tracking it, so I grabbed the phone, turned the volume all the way down on it, took it upstairs to my apartment, and stashed it in a drawer, where I knew that Christine wouldn't look for it. I knew that it would be fine there overnight. It was still risky leaving it at the house, since the cops could have come right to my door anytime, looking for it. But I knew that the chances of that happening were pretty slim.

After stashing the phone, I drove over to Chester's house and bought a forty piece. When I was done smoking it, I went back and bought another one.

In the morning I got up at around nine o'clock and got ready for work. As I was leaving the house, I grabbed the cop's phone from the drawer, and then went down to the car with it.

While I was sitting in the car, waiting for Dave to come down, I turned up the volume on the cop's phone. Unlike the night before and during the period of time before I'd found the phone, the cops were really gabbing. There was a lot of back and forth going on. It was like a big conference call had just started up. From the bit that I heard, it sounded like they were on their way to make a bust.

I decided to just call the cops on the frequency that they were using and get rid of the phone already. I pushed down on the button. "Hey," I said. "Did you guys lose something?"

Immediately, a booming voice came over the radio. "Who is this?" the voice said. "How did you get on this frequency?"

I waited for a few seconds and then pressed down on the button again. "A guy got busted in my car on Friday night," I said. "Some cops searched my car and lost a phone. I just found it. Do you guys want this thing back or not?"

Another cop got on the radio. "Bring it to us," he said. Then he instructed me where to bring it. It was some cop shop downtown.

"No, I don't think so," I said. "I ain't wasting my gas to bring this shit to you guys. I'm not the one who lost it. If you guys want your phone back, you've got to come to me and get it. And you better make it quick, all right? I'm about to leave town. If you guys don't show up in ten minutes, I'm going to chuck it out the window."

"Don't go anywhere," the first cop said. "We'll be right over."

I got out of my car and waited for the cops to show up. It didn't take them long. In less than a couple of minutes, they came pulling into the lot behind my building. And it wasn't just one car that showed up. Two unmarked cars made the trip.

Two plainclothes cops immediately got out of one of the cars and came over to me. I handed them the phone. I assumed that the cops would just take the phone and leave, but they didn't. They started hassling me and asking me for information.

"Let me see your license and registration," one of the cops said.

"Why?" I said. "Did you guys pull me over?"

"No," the cop said.

"That's right. I ain't even in my car right now. I'm standing beside it, on private property. I don't have to give you guys my license and registration. I don't have to give you guys shit!"

"Sir, you don't have to get hostile with us," the other cop said.

"Then quit asking me for information," I said. "You

know, you pigs are lucky that you're even getting this phone back right now. I didn't have to give it back. I could have smashed it onto the fucking pavement. I'm actually saving the city of Hamilton money by giving it back to you guys, so you should be happy with that and fucking beat it."

Both cops immediately backed down. They knew that they had no right to ask me for the shit that they were asking me for. They obviously assumed that I was dumb and that I didn't know my rights.

The cops turned and walked back to their car. Then, as quickly as they'd shown up, they were gone.

20

The day after I returned the cop's phone, Les called me. It was Monday, early in the afternoon, and Christine was at school.

"Hey, Jim, are you busy right now?" Les said.

"No, not really," I said.

"OK. How about we meet, then? I've got some time."

I didn't want to meet with Les, but I figured that I might as well get it over with. "All right," I said. "Where do you want to meet?"

"At the Wendy's on Barton and Centennial," Les said. "I'm there right now. I'm in a grey Ford Taurus. I'm parked on the side of the Wendy's that looks onto Centennial Parkway."

"OK. I'll be there in about fifteen minutes."

I went down to my car and drove over to the Wendy's. When I got there, I parked my car, walked over to Les' car, and got into the passenger seat. Les had a burger wrapper on the dashboard and was finishing up his fries. He took a sip of his drink, put it back into the cup holder, and then pulled a little notebook out of his shirt pocket.

Les opened the notebook and flipped to a fresh page. "I guess that we should get down to business now, eh?" he said.

"OK, what do you want to know?" I said.

"Tell me about Pablo. Who did he buy his dope from?"

"I don't know. I never took him to his dealer's."

"Come on, Jim."

"I'm telling you, man. I don't know."

"OK. Give me someone else, then."

I gave up the name of a crack dealer who I'd heard from Chester and Sal had been busted recently.

"That guy's already been busted," Les said.

"Really?" I said. "I didn't know that."

"Don't jerk me around, Jim."

As much as I wanted to get Les off my ass, I realized that I had no real intention of cooperating with him. Even though he'd threatened me, I just couldn't go through with ratting someone out. I didn't even know for a fact that Les would talk to Christine if I didn't cooperate. For all I knew, it was just an empty threat; an attempt to get me to tell him what he wanted to know.

I decided that the only way to deal with the situation was to give Les some false information. It would get him off my case for a while, I figured, and it would keep him away from Christine. I knew that Les would eventually figure out that what I'd told him was bullshit. If he decided at that point to be a prick and talk to Christine, then I would just have to deal with it. I was planning on telling her the truth at some point anyway.

Les started to tap his pen against his notepad. It was obvious that he was getting impatient with me.

"OK," I said. "I'll give you someone that you don't already know about."

"I'm listening," Les said.

"Ever hear of a guy named Bones?"

The name was kind of stupid, but it wasn't too out there for a street dealer's name. Some dealers used normal-sounding names, but a lot of them, in my experience, used names that were pretty weird.

Les shook his head. "No," he said. "I haven't heard of him. Is he a crack dealer?"

"Yeah," I said.

"White guy?"

"Yeah, he's white."

Les scribbled the name down in his book. "OK," he said. "Where can I find this guy?"

"Downtown," I said. "You know that grassy area on King Street where the war monuments are?"

"Gore Park?"

"Yeah. That's where he hangs out."

"Does he ever hang out anywhere else?"

"I don't know, maybe. I've only bought dope off him a couple of times. I just meet him there and then we walk around the corner and he sells me the dope."

Les scribbled this all down eagerly. "Do you know anyone else?" he said.

"You mean any other crack dealers?" I said.

"Yeah."

"No. Bones is the only guy that I've bought dope from since Pablo got busted."

Les made a couple more notes in his book.

"Are we good now?" I said.

"Yeah, we're good," Les said. "You can go."

I got out of Les' car and walked back over to my car. I waited until Les drove off and then I headed home.

On the way home, I started to feel a little stressed out. I decided to stop by Chester's and get some dope.

A couple of hours after I got high, I went to the university and picked up Christine. After we got home and had supper, I felt like getting high again. I wasn't stressed out about Les anymore or anything. What was done was done. I just felt like getting high because I was bored. Christine had a term paper to work on. I had nothing to do.

I still had some money left from the Woodbine, so I went over to Chester's and got a forty piece. I went home, smoked it, and then cleaned out my stem.

Once I'd cleaned my stem out and the buzz had worn off, I started to feel bored again. Pretty soon, I was jonesing. Since I didn't have any money left, and since driving another crack dealer was obviously out of the question, I decided to just turn to Christine and ask her if she'd lend me sixty bucks.

Christine looked up at me from her computer screen. "Forget it, Jim," she said. "I'm not giving you money so that you can buy weed again."

"Please, baby," I said. "I'll pay you back when I play my first spot."

"You told me yourself that those early spots aren't usually very good. Anyway, you only gave me a hundred and twenty dollars for this month's rent. I can't give you any more money."

Christine went back to her term paper. For the next little while, I sat on the loveseat and said nothing. I just stared at the TV, which was on mute, and tried to get the thought of smoking crack out of my head.

While I sat there, the downstairs neighbours' music thumped beneath the floor. It only put me in a worse mood. It got to the point where I literally wanted to go downstairs and smash their fucking subwoofer in with my baseball bat. That's how irritated I felt.

I finally couldn't take the noise anymore. I grabbed the nearest object—a broken lamp stand that just so happened to be sitting there, at arm's reach—and swung it hard into the floor. It made me feel a bit better, but doing this really freaked out Christine.

"What the hell did you do that for?" Christine said.

"I can't stand listening to this fucking noise anymore," I said. "I had to do something."

"Oh, yeah? And how's that going to solve anything? Are you trying to start something with these people, Jim?"

"Ah, don't worry about it. Just listen."

Downstairs, the neighbours and their friends started laughing and screaming like they were cheering me on.

"See?" I said. "Those drunks fucking liked it. They thought it was funny."

"Why don't you go over to Dave's if you can't stand the noise?" Christine said. "I don't like having to listen to this shit either, but I don't have a choice. I have to get this work done."

"I don't want to go to Dave's. The last time that I went over there, he was fighting with Belinda. They haven't been getting along lately. I don't want to get involved in any of their shit."

"Well, I don't know what to tell you, then."

"How about you just give me a few bucks. I'll chill out and go smoke some weed. I'll pay you back my first day out, I promise. I'll take it out of the apron if I have to."

"How about you wait until your season starts and you

can spend your own money on weed? I already told you, Jim. The answer is no."

I stormed into the kitchen and slammed a couple of cabinet doors shut. It was childish, but I couldn't control myself. I was frustrated.

I went back into the living room and slumped down on the loveseat.

Christine was glaring at me. "Are you going to act like this all night?" she said.

"I don't know," I said. "Maybe."

"Well, stop it, OK? I've got a term paper to finish. I've got to hand it in tomorrow and give a presentation on it to the class. The neighbours are bad enough. I don't need you acting like this right now."

"I don't know why you're making such a big deal out of this, Christine. I told you that I'd pay you back."

Christine fucking lost it. "God, Jim!" she screamed. "What the hell is wrong with you? If I give it to you—if I give you sixty fucking dollars—will you stop acting like this and leave me alone?"

"Yes," I said.

Christine got up and immediately went over to the door. "Come on, then," she said. "Let's go. Get your coat."

I went over to the door, put my coat on, and grabbed my baseball bat. Christine and I went out the back way.

As we walked down the stairs, Christine suddenly noticed the baseball bat in my hand.

"Do you really need to keep carrying that bat around with you?" Christine said. "It's freaking me out, Jim. You told me that the neighbour came up here on Saturday morning and apologized."

"He did," I said. "But I don't trust him. He's a fucking drunk. You never know . . . all of a sudden he could decide to get violent. I just feel safer having the bat."

"So, should I have a bat, then? I feel like I'm going to get attacked now every time that I leave the house."

"Don't be silly."

"How's that silly? You don't even want me to open the door now unless I hear your secret knock."

"That's just a precaution. The neighbour would never mess with you, Christine. This shit is between me and him. He knows that."

Christine didn't look too convinced.

We drove to Centre Mall and Christine took sixty dollars out of the bank machine. She handed me the money and then I drove home to drop her off.

When we got home, Christine got out of the car without saying a word to me. She just slammed the door and hurried up the stairs to the apartment. I wanted to get high so badly that I didn't even care how angry I'd made Christine.

She'll cool off, I told myself, as I drove over to Chester's.

21

At twenty after nine the next morning I drove Christine to the university to hand in her term paper. On the way over there, my brakes started to squeal whenever I braked hard. I realized that my brake pads needed to be replaced immediately, but not having any money, there was nothing that I could do about it. I knew that I would just have to wait until the season started and I'd played at least one good spot.

When we got to the university, Christine gave me a kiss and then got out of the car. Even though she was clearly nervous about the term paper presentation she had to give that day, she was in a much better mood than the night before, when I'd dragged her to the bank machine.

After I'd dropped Christine off, I went home and watched movies all day on my computer. All day I felt edgy and was jonesing to smoke crack.

At around four thirty I drove to the university and picked up Christine. We went home and Christine made supper.

Before supper was ready, my phone rang. I looked at the caller ID. It was an unknown number.

An unpleasant feeling came over me suddenly. I picked up the phone. It was Les.

I was pretty surprised that Les was calling me so soon after meeting with him. I tried to act casual, seeing as how Christine was standing only a few feet away from me, in the kitchen.

"Oh, hey, man," I said. "How's it going?"

"We need to talk," Les said. "You know that name you gave me yesterday? It doesn't check out."

I didn't want to get into any more of a conversation with Les while Christine was in the house. "All right," I said. "Where are you right now? I'll come meet you."

"Let's meet at the Wendy's again," Les said.

"OK. I'll be right over."

I went into the kitchen and put on my coat. Christine had a pot of boiling water on the stove with spaghetti noodles in it.

"Baby, I've got to go out for a bit," I said. "My weed guy wants me to drive him somewhere."

"Oh, OK," Christine said.

I left the house and drove over to the Wendy's. Les was sitting in his Ford Taurus again.

I got into Les' car. Les immediately pulled out his notebook and flipped to the page he'd written on the day before, when we'd met.

"This name you gave me," Les said. "It's bullshit, Jim. No one knows any guy named Bones."

"Are you sure?" I said. "Did you really ask around?"

"Yeah, I'm sure! I was downtown last night and all day today, looking for this guy. Now are you going to cooperate with me here, or should I just go talk to your girlfriend?"

It was at this exact moment that I realized that Les had no real intention of talking to Christine. I clearly hadn't cooperated, yet here he was, continuing to make the same threat he'd made the day before.

I decided to give Les some more false information, just to see how he'd react to it. "OK," I said, pretending to be worried. "I'll give you some names."

"Real ones, this time," Les said.

"Don't worry, these ones are real."

I gave Les a couple of made-up names. He raised his eyebrows and tapped his pen lightly against his notebook as I spoke, but he didn't write any of the information down. It was like he already knew that what I was telling him wouldn't check out.

"What's the matter?" I said, after I'd finished talking. "Aren't you going to write any of this down in your book?"

Les made a couple of quick notes in his book and then quickly flipped the book closed. He glanced at the time on his car stereo and then tucked the book into his shirt pocket. "All right," he said. "Thanks for the info. I've got to get going now, Jim. We'll be in touch."

I nodded, but I was pretty sure this time that I wouldn't ever be hearing from Les again.

I got out of Les' car and watched him take off down Centennial Parkway.

Once Les was out of sight, I walked over to my car, got on the road, and started to drive home.

As I drove, I felt relieved at first. The closer I got to the house, though, the more I started to think about Les and the reason I'd had to meet with him in the first place.

You've got to quit this fucking drug habit, I told myself.

It was April now, anyway. The carnival season was about to start. I knew that once the spots started to get good, once the show that I'd be working for started to play the spring fairs, I'd want to start paying Christine back the money that I owed her for rent, car repairs, and for everything else she'd paid for all winter. I didn't want to have a drug habit anymore draining all my money and making me lie to her all the time.

I got in the door just as Christine finished eating supper.

"Are you going to eat right now?" Christine said. "Or should I put the food away?"

"You can put it away," I said. "I'll eat later."

Christine put the food away. While she was in the kitchen, I went into the bathroom, got my stem, and threw it into the living room garbage can. Then I threw out my X-Acto blade and the thing that I used to push my screen with. The plate that I used when I was cleaning out my stem had some crack residue on it. As soon as Christine got out of the kitchen, I went in there and scrubbed the plate with soap and water.

After getting rid of all of my crack stuff, I felt a bit better. I went into the living room and watched some TV with the volume turned down low, while Christine worked on her last stats assignment.

Pretty soon, I started jonesing. The craving came on extremely strong. I wanted so badly to ask Christine for money to buy a forty piece, but I managed to restrain myself. To do this, I literally had to physically remove myself from the apartment and go for a walk.

I walked all around the neighbourhood, but it did nothing to clear my head. I was still jonesing. I was thinking about smoking crack so much that it was literally making me fart and feel like I was going to shit myself, almost as if I'd just scored some dope and I was on my way home to smoke it.

Somehow I managed to get through the rest of the night without getting high. I barely slept at all. It was pure willpower that stopped me from rolling over in bed and asking Christine if she'd let me drag her to the bank machine again at two o'clock in the morning. My stem was still in the living room garbage can. I could have easily retrieved it and then smoked the forty piece in the bathroom.

In the morning I got up and drove Christine to the university. When I got home later, I decided to call up a couple of shows that I knew of. Even though the Woodbine was pretty good money for a couple days' work, it wasn't enough work. I needed to finally get a hole for the season.

One of the show owners that I called was this guy named Jesse Macdonald. Right away, Jesse offered me a job in his balloon store for the season. I immediately thought about Dave.

"Hey, I've got a buddy who needs a hole, too," I said. "Have you got anything for him?"

"Is he a good agent?" Jesse said.

"Yeah, man. Dave Connolly."

"Oh, yeah, I know Davey. How's he been?"

"All right."

"Well, I've got a star dart game that he could work in. We've got a spot this weekend. If he's interested, let me know, Jimmy."

I went over to Dave's place as soon as I got off the phone with Jesse. Dave was in the middle of another poker tournament. Thankfully, Belinda was out shopping. Dave and I smoked a joint while I told him about the hole I'd gotten him for the season.

"Doesn't Jesse play all those spots out in the middle of nowhere?" Dave said.

"Yeah," I said. "So?"

"So, I want to come home on my days off, Jim. I want to spend time with Belinda."

"Dave, I've got a car. I'll make sure that you get home on your days off so that you can see Belinda. The question is do you want to come out with me? There's a spot this weekend. I already got you a hole."

"Where'd you say this spot was again?"

"Burlington. It's a Canadian Tire parking lot."

"Hmmph."

"Dave, it's their first spot of the season. What do you expect? It'll probably still be as good as the Woodbine. It might even be better if we get good weather."

I couldn't believe what a dick Dave was being. I'd gotten him a hole for the season and here he was, turning his nose up at it.

"I'm kind of thinking of going back to work for Herlahey this year," Dave said.

"*Herlahey*?" I said.

Jack Herlahey was a bastard show owner who'd ripped me and Dave off for a few grand at the Canadian National Exhibition in Toronto one year. It was the same year, actually, that I'd met Christine there, when she'd had a job there, doing the breaks and stocking the joints for a guy who just hired university students. I couldn't imagine how Dave could ever consider working for that jag, Herlahey, ever again, unless it was to rob him. But I knew that Dave wouldn't do that. He didn't even steal as much from the apron as I did.

"What the hell do you want to work for Herlahey for?" I

said. "Don't you remember how he ripped us off?"

"He plays a lot of spots in the GTA," Dave said.

"I already told you, Dave. Don't worry about that shit. If you work for Jesse, I'll make sure that you get home on your days off."

Dave still wouldn't give me a definite answer. "I'll have to run it by Belinda first," he said. "She should be home soon."

I rolled my eyes. Since when did you become such a bitch? I thought.

"Do what you want," I said. "If you hem and haw over this too much, though, Dave, you're going to miss out on the opportunity."

"OK," Dave said. "Tell Jesse I'm in. When do we open?"

"Friday at four."

I sat around and watched Dave play poker for a while. He got eliminated from the tournament and then, shortly after that, Belinda came home from shopping. That was my cue to leave. I got up from the couch, muttered hello to Belinda, and then went back to my place.

When I got home, I called Jesse back and told him that Dave wanted to work for him in the star dart for the season. Jesse told me that he needed our help setting up a few joints the next morning. We also needed to stock the joints that we would be working in, or flash them, as we called it.

I called Dave to let him know about the set-up. I told him that he needed to be ready to leave at around nine thirty in the morning.

"OK," Dave said.

"You better not stay up all night, playing poker," I said.

"Don't worry. I won't."

That night I had another really crappy sleep. I was still

getting extremely intense cravings to smoke crack. I managed not to cave in, though. I didn't ask Christine for any money. I was actually pretty proud of myself.

In the morning I went to Burlington with Dave for set-up. The set-up went pretty fast. By two thirty in the afternoon, we were out of there.

Dave had a poker tournament that he wanted to play when we got back to Hamilton, so I went back to my place. Christine was taking a nap in the bedroom when I got home.

I made something quick to eat—a baloney and cheese sandwich. Just as I sat down to eat it, I got a call from Theresa, my worker.

"The fraud department finished conducting their investigation," Theresa told me. "We're releasing a cheque to you today, Jim. You can pick it up, or we can mail it."

Seeing as what had happened the last time welfare had mailed a cheque out to me, I didn't want them to do that again.

"Please don't mail it," I said. "I'll come pick it up today."

"OK, we close at four thirty," Theresa said.

"I'll come over right now. I'll be there in a few minutes."

I was so happy that I was finally going to get my welfare cheque. It was about damn time.

I hung up the phone, put my sandwich in the fridge, and threw on my jacket. Then I went into the bedroom and woke up Christine to tell her that I'd gotten home from work, but that I was going out again.

"I'll be back in a little while, OK?" I said. "I'm just going over to the welfare office."

"Are they giving you your cheque, finally?" Christine said.

"That's what my worker told me over the phone."

I drove to the welfare office and met with Theresa. We went into her office and she gave me my cheque and had me sign for it.

Once I'd signed for my cheque, Theresa saw me out to the lobby.

"Don't forget to turn in your card later this month if you need to continue collecting Ontario Works," Theresa said.

"OK, thanks," I said.

I had no intention of handing in another card to welfare, though. Even though I knew that I'd probably be working under the table for Jesse, in which case I could have continued to collect welfare without welfare ever finding out about it, I didn't want to do that. I never liked being on welfare unless I really needed it. It was also a pain in the ass having to turn in that card every month.

I left the welfare office and drove to the TD bank at Centre Mall. I cashed my cheque and then paid my car insurance.

I left the bank with the intention of going home and giving Christine a hundred and thirty bucks to put towards the rent that I still owed her for April. As I got into my car, though, something strange happened. I was suddenly overcome by these horrible thoughts:

What if the spot this weekend turns out to be a total blank? What if it rains the whole weekend?

The first couple of spots of the season weren't that great, usually. They were mainly for the show to get the rides set up and to make sure that everything was operating properly. If the weather was bad, I knew that I wouldn't make much money at the Canadian Tire parking lot in Burlington. I didn't want to give Christine money off my welfare cheque and then have to ask for it back, like I'd done the whole winter, basically, whenever I needed to fill up or buy a pack of smokes. My phone bill would be due soon. I needed to have some money to pay it. It was better not to give Christine any money then to ask for it back, I felt.

I drove to a convenience store and bought a pack of smokes. Then, as much as I hated myself for doing it, I went to Chester's to buy a forty piece. I told myself, though, as I drove over there, that this was going to be my last one. I was going to go home and smoke it, and then that was going to be it.

I got home with the dope, just as Christine was getting up from her nap.

"How did it go at the welfare office?" Christine said.

"Ah, it was bullshit," I said. "My worker just wanted me to come in and sign some more papers. I have no idea when they're actually going to give me my cheque."

"I thought you said that your worker was going to release a cheque to you today."

"That's what I thought she said. I guess I misheard."

"Oh, well. At least your season is starting now, honey. I wouldn't worry about it."

Christine sat down on the couch and started to do some marking. She had a stack of term papers to mark for the undergraduate course she was TA'ing for. The stack was about a foot high.

While Christine was distracted, marking papers, I fished my crack stem out of the living room garbage can. Then I went into the bathroom to get high.

When I was done getting high, it was around suppertime. Christine took a break from her marking and started to make supper.

Twenty minutes later, I could smell food cooking on the stove. It made me feel terrible. I knew that I wasn't going to eat anything because I was coming down now and wasn't hungry. Christine would have to put my portions into containers and then put them in the fridge.

What a waste of effort, I thought.

I looked at the stack of term papers on the coffee table that Christine had to get through and then thought about how hard she'd been working all winter and how broke she now was. I started to feel bad about not telling her that I'd gotten my welfare cheque, and about the whole winter, honestly.

You've got to make it up to her as soon as the spots start getting good and you start making some real money, I told myself.

The smells from the kitchen started to get stronger. I started to feel worse.

You've got to make it up to her soon . . .

Made in the USA
Charleston, SC
26 February 2016